# Unaccompanied Minor

One man's journey from bystander to
anti-child trafficking activist

Kitania Kavey & Claire Nagel

*Based on the screenplay*
*Unaccompanied Minor*
*by Kitania Kavey*

Published by BookLocker.com, Inc., St. Petersburg, Florida.

Unaccompanied Minor is a work of fiction. The incidents, dialogue, and all characters, with the exception of Rob Waterlander, are products of the author's imaginations or used fictitiously. However, child trafficking is not fictitious. For more information, there are organizations dedicated to recognizing and stopping child trafficking using airlines, as well as general anti-trafficking organizations located worldwide.

Printed on acid-free paper.

Booklocker.com, Inc.
2019

First Edition

# Chapter One

Rob wasn't a man prone to introspection. It was not like him to brood like this as he sat stiffly, waiting for his next transport client.

He watched holiday travelers swarm through the airport, undeterred by the icy, windy weather outside which threatened to delay flights. Normally he felt at ease in the maze of cavernous white-tiled concourses lined with shops and glass walls that showcased the runways. Today the duty-free shops were garishly decorated with Christmas-themed displays that made the overcast gray day outside seem even more dismal to him.

Rob's electric cart was parked across from the gate where a flight from Delhi was due to arrive. He sat up a little straighter, as if that might strengthen him against his emotional disquiet. He wanted very much to return to his usual calm, detached state. But that glimpse of a young girl skipping down the concourse kept popping back into his mind. She looked so like his daughter – at least how she had looked a few years ago. Maaika had always been daddy's girl, greeting him each time he returned home with exuberant smiles and kisses. He missed her so much.

It had all fallen apart, the family he'd assumed would always be there. His life was quite different back then. He worked in construction, handling sales. That job afforded him a nice lifestyle. Sure, it kept him on the road a lot, but it more than paid the bills. It never occurred to him that his wife was not satisfied. After all, he'd bought her a house and didn't complain all that much about her frequent spending sprees.

Then, out of the blue, she left him for a man who could buy her a bigger house, even more baubles, more shoes, more skirts and blouses and dresses and jewelry and other frippery. The worst of it was that she had taken his children, luring them away with promises of more stuff. His son was a bit older then, just starting high school, and a carbon copy of his wife - easily seduced by the prestige money could give him with his shallow friends.

4

While his son had gone along with his mother and refused to have contact with him, Maaika, who still had the angelic innocence of a child, wanted to keep in touch. They had exchanged emails and the occasional call at first, but his ex-wife finally managed to drive a wedge between them and all contact had stopped. Somehow she made it seem that the family falling apart was entirely Rob's fault. He had not paid enough attention to her or the children, spent too much time away from home, didn't provide enough luxuries, and on and on. Now he had not seen his children in over two years! He felt like he was missing a piece of his soul, and today that loss weighed on him even more than it normally did.

He tried again to rein in his thoughts. The ruling on their contentious divorce had favored his wife, who sold the family home and kept custody of the kids. He moved out and gave up his old job, trying in his own way for a fresh start. He'd been good at sales once, but after the divorce, his self-confidence was shattered. He closed himself off and had tried to shutter his emotions in order to get through each day since then.

Now he had a small but decent apartment and a job as a passenger assistant that suited him fairly well, except for the money, of course. But with only himself to provide for, it was adequate. By adhering to a strict budget and living a simple lifestyle, he had even managed to put aside a few extra Euros.

His job required only that he be competent and reliable, and cordial during the time it took to ferry his clients from one part of the airport to another. He could slip cordiality on like a raincoat when it was required, and peel it off again when it was no longer needed. Since there was a strict no-tipping policy, he didn't have to worry about schmoozing, he could just keep everything cool and polite.

Rob found the work satisfactory, and his performance reviews were decent. For the rest, he had built up a wall around his emotions, and had long ago stopped trying to analyze what had gone wrong in his marriage. The only thing that he couldn't mute was the guilt that maybe he could have done something differently.

The flight from Delhi arrived and there was no time now to continue brooding over the past. Rob smoothed his unwrinkled uniform and straightened his I.D. badge. Nearing his fifties, he had held on to a trim physique.

Time had worn a few lines into his face, but he kept his head shaved smooth to conceal a receding hairline and graying hair. He looked okay for his age; in fact, his only complaint was that he was shorter than average. One might not have noticed his height in another country, but the Netherlands generally had a taller population than the rest of the world. Nevertheless, he didn't stand out in a crowd for reasons either good or bad, and that suited him just fine.

The ground staff only paid attention to his uniform and I.D. badge, which was clearly visible hanging from a cord around his neck. They waved him through without a word. Rob entered the plane to pick up an unaccompanied minor, glancing at his PDA to check the details: a ten-year-old girl, Naima Gupta. He'd best be prepared for a cranky kid after such a long flight.

The blue seats with bright red accents filling the cabin did nothing to chase away the somber weather glowering through every window. Rob caught the attention of the head stewardess in the central galley. He'd worked with Anna before and found her to be efficient. She was well-kept and pleasant enough to look at, but the Nordic type did not interest him. Since his divorce, he hadn't been interested in anyone.

"You've got a U.M. for me?" He didn't bother with polite formalities, and reserved idle pleasantries for the clients.

"Yes, a young lady." Anna was a multi-tasker and also economical with words. She handed him the girl's documents and gestured towards the rear of the cabin.

There were a few remaining passengers who were still retrieving luggage from the overhead bins.

Rob craned his neck to see past the stragglers to the spot Anna had indicated. That had to be her – the exotic-looking kid clutching a small pink backpack. She was sitting silently with her eyes closed, and looked younger than ten. He checked the documents in his hand to confirm the girl's passport and information were in good order.

Anna touched his sleeve and changed her tone to sound a bit warmer. "It's Rob, isn't it? Could you do me a favor?" She smiled automatically, as she had to thousands of passengers on hundreds of flights, a smile that didn't reach her cool blue eyes and icy blonde hair.

"Sure." He was still thinking that the girl looked younger than ten.

"There's an older woman who also needs assistance. Would you mind? I'll bring her to you."

It wasn't said as a question, really, and Rob answered, "No problem," only out of habit.

Anna had already moved off towards the front of the plane, and Rob approached the child at the rear. She was thin, but her face still held the roundness of baby fat. She had thick dark hair, worn in a single loose braid. She sat very still, but somehow seemed to be at attention, her body in no way relaxed or slumped as one might expect from a sleeping child. "Hi there, Naima. I'm Rob."

As he spoke her name, her eyes flew open. They dominated her face, huge and black. And full of... fear. Thinking he had startled her, he reached out a hand and said, "It's all right, I'm here to take you to your family."

She stared at him for a moment. She had a dreamy look about her, as though she were half-asleep. Perhaps she had been asleep and had a nightmare?

Rob continued to hold out his hand in what he hoped was a non-threatening manner. Neither of them moved, and the sound of the wind blustering outside seemed to fill the cabin. Then, resignedly, she took his hand and stood up. She wore a short denim skirt and a light jacket more suitable for a tropical climate.

"Is your carry-on in the overhead bin?"

She appeared puzzled by his question. He almost always chose to speak in English instead of Dutch, and while he had conversational ability in German and French, he doubted either would be helpful if she only spoke one of the Indian dialects.

"Do you have a suitcase? How about a coat?" He made a few pantomimes to try to make things clearer for her.

She shook her head and clutched her backpack. She shook her head even more vehemently when Rob offered to carry it for her. Hopefully she at least understood his intentions.

He took a step back and she moved unsteadily into the aisle ahead of him. Surely she must have brought more with her than just the little backpack. He could see there was a design on it, some sort of animal character. As he ushered her toward the exit he was reminded of Maaika's first day of school, so long ago now. She had also worn a little backpack, black with a red ladybug on it, from what he recalled.

*Naima wanted to run, to try once more to escape, but she sensed that this was not the time.*

*The fear welled up again. She'd been walking home from the potato fields where she had done a good day's work. She'd been proud of herself. She had harvested eight big bags! Soon she would be home and helping her mother prepare the family supper. Sure, she was tired, but she was happy.*

*She didn't think much of it as the car approached down the dusty road until it pulled up alongside her. Without warning, a man came out of the car, grabbed her, clapped his hand over her mouth and dragged her into the car. She'd struggled, but then there was the prick in her arm. Things were pretty hazy from then on.*

*There was a long car ride, confusing images of city streets, and confinement in a small room. There was a mean, angry-looking woman telling her with gestures that she must eat the plate of strange food and drink the bitter tea provided once a day. Pure terror as a man's rough hands pushed her legs apart, and then the pain. Later—how much later?—another car ride. The woman dragging her along through the airport where everyone spoke a language she did not understand.*

*Finally on the plane, and blessedly alone for the first time in many days, she'd slept as much as she could, waking only to eat the food brought by the nice woman in the pretty uniform.*

*As her mind began to feel less foggy, she figured out that it had been the bitter tea that made her feel so confused and out of it. If she was ever going to be able to escape she would need to think clearly. So she hid two bottles of water and a couple packages of snacks in her backpack. For now, she would play along and pretend she was still the sleepy, obedient little girl.*

When they reached the galley area, Anna had already returned with a very short, slightly rotund Indian woman dressed in a beautiful sari. She had a winter coat under one arm and was clutching a can of soda along with her large purse in the other. A well-worn carry-on suitcase rested at her feet. "Mrs. Leek, this is Rob. He will make sure you get through customs, help you get your luggage and escort you to your waiting party."

Mrs. Leek smiled up at Rob coquettishly, then, noticing the child, bent down and spoke to her sweetly in rapid Hindi. Naima just stood there mutely, still looking half-asleep. Rob wondered if Naima understood anything going on around her, and hoped the pantomiming would keep working, especially if Mrs. Leek also wasn't fluent in English.

Rob nodded a cursory goodbye to Anna, picked up Mrs. Leek's carry-on and shepherded her and Naima off of the plane and to his cart. Mrs. Leek settled herself immediately into the front passenger seat, so Naima climbed automatically into the back seat, hanging tightly onto her backpack. Rob loaded the luggage, slipped into the driver's seat and took off smoothly.

The whole time Mrs. Leek kept up a steady stream of chatter. Since it was all in Hindi, Rob had no idea what she was saying, so he just nodded occasionally as he wove expertly through the airport. Naima also seemed not to understand a word that was said. That apparently didn't bother Mrs. Leek one bit. She was cheerful and animated all the way through customs and baggage claim, a sharp contrast to Naima, who barely looked up and never uttered a word.

They left the electric cart at customs and proceeded on foot. Passenger Assistants could bring their clients to a priority customs agent, thus avoiding the long lines. Rob showed Naima's passport to the agent who gave it a cursory glance and a stamp. Mrs. Leek was also ushered through without delay. There was an extra fee for passenger assistance, but the convenience was well worth it.

Rob now carried Mrs. Leek's coat and small suitcase and he picked up a huge wheeled suitcase for her in baggage claim. Even with the crush of travelers he was adept at finding his way through the chaos without incident. He also managed to keep an eye on Naima, who followed closely, eyes downcast. She still had only her backpack, as she'd had no luggage to collect.

They wended their way through the throng towards arrivals, where a slew of welcoming families and friends waited excitedly. Suddenly, Mrs. Leek shrieked and waddled swiftly toward a large group of Indian folks who were waving wildly. She had found her family.

Rob watched with a benign smile as the family embraced Mrs. Leek and showered her with kisses. He handed over her coat and suitcases, and then turned his attention to his other charge.

"It's Naima, right?" He tried to sound fatherly, comforting, but the child just stood there, clutching her backpack to her chest. He checked the paperwork again. Something still didn't feel right. This kid was too quiet. And where was her winter clothing, her luggage? He squatted down beside her. "Naima. Am I saying it right?" She nodded, eyes still downcast. Maybe she did get a few words in English. Rob tried again, remembered what was written on her UM form, but not sure if he would be able to pantomime what he wanted to ask. "Is your sister here to pick you up?"

That seemed to get her attention. She looked up and began to survey the crowd. When she saw two people step slightly forward and begin to wave toward Rob, she pulled back. She looked into Rob's eyes with what he interpreted as both fear and resignation. Still, she said nothing and Rob could only squat there as the throng moved around them.

His back was slightly to the welcoming crowd, and he was able to surreptitiously recheck Naima's paperwork before he stood up. He was still facing Naima, but could see the couple in his peripheral vision.

The woman looked to be in her thirties and was bordering on obese, with a pale complexion and beady eyes. Her winter coat was grubby and seemed to be a style from a decade ago. Her makeup was gaudy and applied with a heavy hand, which did nothing to improve her appearance. The man with her was short, swarthy, and shifty-eyed, and kept himself partially concealed behind his partner.

The woman drew a piece of paper from her pocket, glanced at it, nodded to herself and then beckoned again to Rob. "Oi, 'ere we are," she called out. Her voice sounded brash and a bit too loud even in the din that filled the arrivals hall. She had a distinctly British accent, which in itself wasn't unusual in a Dutch airport, but it nevertheless rubbed Rob the wrong way for no reason he could put his finger on.

Rob took Naima's hand without thinking and together they walked slowly toward the strange couple. There was no way these two characters could be related to Naima, but his paperwork mentioned a pickup from a sister. He tried to keep his misgivings out of his voice. "Hello, I'm Rob. I work for the Passenger Assistant Services. Are you Bertha Robbins, Naima's sister?"

"'At's me, love."

"May I see your ID, please?"

This woman who could not possibly be Naima's sister, handed him an ID. He carefully matched the name on the card to his paperwork. "Okay, thanks." He returned the ID card. His job was done.

The swarthy man with the shifty eyes reached out and pulled Naima close, away from Rob. It was definitely not a welcoming hug. More like taking possession. Naima did not resist, but kept her eyes on Rob. Was she trying to tell him something? What should he do? Wanting to stall for just a little more time, Rob asked, "Naima didn't have any luggage checked?"

Bertha seemed to be about to answer, but was cut off by her companion.

"No." said the man belligerently. His voice matched his gruff exterior.

"Just a short visit, then?" Rob knew he was overstepping his bounds, but the words just slipped out before he could stop them.

Bertha attempted to maneuver her bulk to block off more of the swarthy man and Naima from Rob's view, but they were all still standing closely, confined by the crowds around them. Rob caught a whiff of Bertha's unpleasant, sweaty body odor that she had attempted to conceal with some cheap body spray.

"Oh, no," Bertha declared. "She'll be 'ere a while. She can use my things." The swarthy man gave her a nasty look and Bertha stopped talking abruptly.

"I see." Rob tried to wipe the puzzled look off his face. He could not see how this chubby woman's clothes could possibly fit tiny Naima. Maybe the backpack contained all the toiletries a young girl might need, but certainly there wasn't room for even a couple of changes of winter clothes. For goodness sake, the child's shoes were what looked like hand-me-down sandals, completely unfit for the weather outside.

"Is that all then?" snapped the man as he draped his jacket over Naima's thin shoulders. He glared at everything but Rob, never directly making eye contact. His voice also had an accent, but it hinted at an Eastern European origin, definitely not British. His fingers pinned his jacket tightly around Naima's shoulders and Rob could see that, unexpectedly, the man's hands were baby-smooth with clean and well-manicured nails.

Rob could not think of a way to stall any longer. He leaned over towards Naima. He really wanted to scoop her up and take her away from these unsettling people, but all he could think of to do was say, "Nice meeting you, Naima." He hoped that she could hear him over the din and that she would understand. He was confused by his feeling of uneasiness and he had already breached the carefully controlled assistant/client code of conduct.

Naima's gaze dropped and she allowed herself to be pulled away. Rob stood stock still and watched as this implausible trio merged into the undulating crowd.

Then a voice interrupted his pensive thoughts. "Excuse me, I seem to have missed my party. Is it possible I could make an announcement over the loudspeaker?"

A neatly-dressed businessman required his attention. Inwardly Rob tried to silence his thoughts while he jolted his body into action. He pasted a generic, polite smile on his face. "Sure, come with me, please." After a final glance toward where he had last seen Naima, Rob got back to the distractions of normal work. Nonetheless, for the rest of his shift and all the way on the train ride home, he could not get the sight of the terrified little girl out of his mind.

He knew there was something wrong. That woman could not possibly be Naima's sister. And that man - he'd never have allowed a man like that to touch his daughter. It made his skin crawl.

*Naima kept up her pretended sleepiness as they walked through the airport. As soon as they stepped out into the wintry blast, she began to shiver. She had never experienced anything like this cold. Her thin little shoes and denim skirt afforded no warmth.*

*Several times as they walked what seemed like forever across the parking lot to a car she stumbled and would have fallen had the nasty man not painfully jerked her upright. He unlocked the car and roughly pushed her into the back seat. He got in the driver's seat and the lady got in the front seat beside him.*

*As the car began to warm up and her teeth stopped chattering, Naima assessed her situation. The car door appeared to be locked. How to open it? If she did figure that out, could she open it, jump out and run away fast enough to escape? But then what?*

Rob was still adrift in his thoughts when he arrived home. The orderliness and simplicity of his apartment usually had a soothing effect on him. Some people might call it stark or even sterile, but it suited him perfectly. There were no pictures to remind him of his former life, to cause the bitterness to rise in his throat. It was a place of calm, if not really of peace, with walls as blank as he wished his mind to be.

Tonight, however, as he prepared his dinner he kept thinking about Naima. She had pierced the armor he had so carefully built up to shield himself from the pain, anger, and resentment that simmered beneath the surface, trapped there by past events. His body made dinner automatically, while he berated himself in his head.

"Put the kid out of your mind. You did your job. It's none of your business. Nothing you can do anyway. So what if that Bertha clearly wasn't blood-related to Naima? But the child had no winter clothing, and there was no way she could possibly use Bertha's clothes. What was this woman doing here, passing herself off as Naima's sister? STOP! Pull yourself together! You checked the documentation. The papers were all in good order. It's NONE of your business."

Although he had not really convinced himself, Rob finished his supper and picked up a book on nutrition he had begun last week. It did not quite accomplish the purpose of quieting his mind, so he put it aside and instead prepared for bed. Routine always helped to settle him.

Finally under his covers with the sound of the wind muffled, he had the feeling he was wrapped in a cocoon, insulated and at last, quiet. The shell he had so carefully crafted was back in place.

# Chapter Two

When Rob awoke, he found the weather had not improved. The morning skies were gray and threatening. He dressed in jeans and a long-sleeved tee-shirt under a thick sweater. It was warm enough in his apartment, but the wan light that filtered through the windows made him feel chilly.

He retrieved the day's newspaper and sat down to his customary breakfast of organic tea, brown bread, and cheese. He didn't often work out, but kept himself in good form with healthy eating habits. He wasn't vain; he just enjoyed feeling fit for his age.

He skimmed idly through the newspaper. There were the usual stories of international unrest and local politicians squabbling over inconsequential issues, warnings of dire weather to come, and ads promoting the upcoming holidays. None of it was of particular interest to Rob. Reading the morning paper was just a habit, part of the routine that kept him from thinking about his sorry life. He really didn't care about what was happening in the stock market or the latest escapades of celebrities and VIPs.

Nothing in the headlines caught his attention until he saw a small article on page five. The headline read "Child Found Dead in Canal."

Rob stared at the accompanying images. One was of the location; the other was an artist's sketch to get the public's help in identifying the young girl. She looked eerily like his U.M. from yesterday. The article said there was no identification, but the child appeared to be eight or ten years old, with a medium complexion and dark hair and eyes. She was wearing a lightweight jacket and skirt, not normal winter clothing. There were no missing persons reports, and authorities did not yet know whether her death was the result of an accident or foul play.

Rob stared hard at the sketch until there was no doubt in his mind. It was Naima. He'd known there was something wrong, but he hadn't said anything, hadn't done anything. He'd just let that weird couple take her away, and now she was dead and no one even knew her name. Come to think of it, he couldn't remember her full name.

Shock, guilt, and sadness swirled through his mind. He couldn't stand it. He had to tell someone. He picked up his cell phone and dialed his work colleague Samir, who was the closest thing to a friend Rob had. He knew Samir was probably at the airport– if anyone worked more than he did, it was Sam– and he'd have access to the passenger assistants' scheduling system.

Once Samir was on the line, Rob jumped right in. "Sam, do me a favor. Look up my U.M. from yesterday afternoon. I picked up a girl on the flight from Allahabad and Delhi. I need to know her full name."

Samir, bless him, didn't ask any questions. After the briefest of pauses he said, "Sure, man. Here it is. Ten-year-old girl, Naima Gupta. Being picked up by a sister."

"Yes, that's the one. Sam, she's dead. There's a picture in the newspaper. The article says her identity is unknown. But I'm sure it's the same kid." Rob could hear the din of the airport over the phone as Samir left the office and entered the main hall.

"You're kidding, right? You must be mistaken. It's pretty busy here, man. Are you scheduled to work today? Maybe we can talk then."

"Yes, I'm in this afternoon." He could tell that Samir was distracted and not really paying attention.

Samir bade him a cheery "Catch you then," and they hung up.

Samir was a friend, even though he was much younger and sometimes seemed like he didn't take anything in life that seriously. Rob didn't know what he was expecting; maybe that Samir would at least have had time to listen. But that was a futile thought, given the extra holiday air traffic and poor weather.

Samir believed that any situation could be improved by going out to a nightclub to dance or by meeting women, and that there was always someone else to take responsibility for the more serious things in life. He still lived at home where his mom cooked and cleaned for him, and as a serial dater, he was unlikely to settle down or move out anytime soon.

Maybe Sam was right. Was he imagining the resemblance in the newspaper? This time of year was especially difficult, as his own family memories returned to the forefront of his mind. Could it be possible that he was mistaken?

Rob sat and stared at the picture. He could not take his eyes off it. This was certainly the little girl he'd escorted through the airport only yesterday. She had been so quiet and sleepy looking. And, yes, he had seen the terror in her eyes, but he'd closed his mind to it and done his job. That's all he was supposed to do, right?

Images of the couple who had picked up Naima floated through Rob's mind; the slovenly woman who claimed to be her sister and the swarthy guy who had grabbed Naima so roughly. No winter clothing, no luggage. He had felt there was something very wrong. But the paperwork was all in good order. What should he have done? More to the point, what could he do now?

Rob got up and busied himself washing up his few breakfast dishes and straightening up his already orderly apartment. Everything had its place, neat and tidy. There was nothing to disturb the calm surface that covered the pain and turmoil and guilt that roiled beneath the surface. He'd kept it all in check for the past couple of years, and had been doing well.

He liked his current job. His old sales job had been a different story. It was commission-based and he had been under constant pressure from both his wife and his boss to earn a lot and get ahead. Now he no longer had the strain of meeting sales quotas or having to hard-sell indifferent potential clients. Working at the airport as a passenger assistant satisfied his ingrained desire to help those in need, and during every shift he felt like he was capable and competent, which at the very least did not further erode his self-confidence.

He didn't have to think about what went before or what would happen to those folks after they left his care. He just had to get them quickly and safely through customs and baggage claim or on to their next flight. They drifted through his life with nary a ripple.

Well, yesterday's unaccompanied minor sure caused more than a ripple. Rob was shaken to the core. The argument in his head made him feel guilty for not doing anything, and angry that there was nothing logical that he could have done. Somewhere buried under the guilt he felt powerless, less manly. Since his divorce, he had become much less assertive and sometimes felt like he was barely hanging on to the appearance of self-control.

Rob's natural, inbred caution came to the rescue. He would not do anything rash; just take one step at a time, follow protocol and the chain of command. At least he now had the girl's full name. Could he be helpful with that?

Rob looked at the news article and picture again and decided on his course of action. He changed his clothes and carefully buttoned his blue uniform, making sure his shoes were properly shined with everything ship-shape. He glanced out the window at the weather and realized he'd best exchange his dress shoes for boots.

In a few minutes, he was ready for work and prepared to brave the elements. That at least he was sure he could do well. He squared his shoulders, checked that he had his keys and his PDA, and stepped out of his apartment. He locked the door methodically and started the short walk to the train station.

He appeared outwardly to be his usual calm, if somewhat detached, self. Only the most astute observer would have seen evidence of the turmoil he was steadfastly suppressing. He had deliberately left his newspaper at home. No sense in scratching the itch.

Even though his train was running a few minutes late because of the weather, he still managed to arrive a few minutes early for his shift.

When he entered the Passenger Assistant Services office, schedulers were busy at their computer terminals as passenger assistants in their blue uniforms scurried back and forth.

Rob traversed the office and entered the break room. His friend Samir followed a moment later, eager to hear the story. "So, tell me."

"I have to keep it short; my shift starts in five. I picked up the girl yesterday morning and they pulled her dead body from the canal last night."

"That's weird, man. Are you sure it's the same girl?"

"It was her."

Samir put his hand on Rob's shoulder in sympathy, but then, distracted, nodded hello to a pair of colleagues canoodling surreptitiously in the corner. Rumor had it they had moved in together. Samir had introduced them.

Rob tried to draw back Samir's attention. "They found her without I.D. The police don't know if it was an accident, but..." Rob shook his head, looked at his feet and then sadly into Samir's kind, dark brown eyes.

"Tragic. I'm sure they'll figure it out. This is really hitting you hard, isn't it?"

"Of course! She is--was just a kid."

"Yeah, man. But it's not your fault. Why take on blame for something that's not your responsibility?"

Maybe Samir was right, but Rob couldn't see it. Emotions he couldn't control were piling up just under the surface. "She didn't have any luggage, and no winter clothing," he blurted out, as if that somehow explained everything.

Samir furrowed his brow and said, "It sounds like a sad situation, but it's no business of ours. Let it go."

Samir reached out again to touch Rob's shoulder, attempting a reassuring gesture, but Rob brushed it off with a curt, "I have to go."

Samir had good intentions, but a comforting pat was not what Rob wanted. What he really wanted was to have someone validate his feelings of outrage, anger and yes, guilt. He saw Samir shrug, unburdened by Rob's concerns, as he easily moved on to another conversation about work and gossip. Always smiling and charming, Samir seemed to not have a care in the world, confident that someone else would deal with the more serious issues in life. Rob envied that.

Even if he could go back and start yesterday over, he still didn't know what he should have done differently, and that bothered him immensely. That he couldn't just figure it out himself reminded him of how often he felt weak and inadequate. He took a deep breath, forcing his thoughts to quiet. He still had a couple minutes until his shift started.

Rob made his way out of the break room and down a hall towards the manager's office. He normally had very little contact with Jan de Graaf. There was no need since Rob was a good worker who followed the rules and took his job seriously. He was reliable and punctual. He had never had an issue before. Even now he could just turn around and go about his shift quietly, let it go as Sam had suggested.

But staff had been encouraged to speak with their superiors if there ever was a problem, and assured that there would be help to resolve whatever the issue was. And he was too stubborn to let it go, so he continued down the hall.

Jan de Graaf 's job was to manage the Passenger Assistant Services program so that clients were served in a timely fashion with courtesy and respect. The program was a subcontractor of the airport, so he had to make sure there were no problems on that front either. Ruffle feathers on either side and the airport could easily replace them with another subcontractor. Jan had a small office with a large window that overlooked a row of parked airplanes.

Jan's door was almost always left open as a signal that he was available to help deal with any problems that might arise. Like any good manager, he knew just enough about the men and women who worked for him so he could anticipate and avert problems. He knew which women had kids prone to sickness and were therefore likely to cause scheduling problems, and which young men on the prowl might need to be reminded of the company's policies to never get too friendly with a client.

From Jan's perspective, Rob was close to an ideal employee – almost always willing to take an extra shift, come in early or stay late. He knew Rob had been through a nasty divorce and lost contact with his children, but that did not seem to affect his performance. If he was not Mr. Cheerful, at least he was always courteous, and had never reported any issues or problems before. So Jan was surprised when Rob knocked on his open door.

"Excuse me, do you have a moment?"

Jan beckoned him in to take a seat, but continued to type into his computer, anticipating nothing serious. "Yes, of course."

Rob sat down, unsure whether to close the door behind him. "Something happened yesterday."

"Oh, was there a problem?"

"A U.M. arrival that I had yesterday is dead."

Jan stopped typing and gave Rob his full attention. "What?"

"The police think she might have been killed, and I had a bad feeling."

"Close the door." Once Rob had returned to his seat, Jan continued, "Tell me exactly what you are talking about."

"I picked up a girl yesterday, inbound from India, along with an elderly lady from the same flight. It was busy. The girl didn't have any luggage. Her sister picking her up didn't look anything like her. It just felt wrong somehow." Rob knew he was not telling the story well. He was not getting across what was so wrong about the way it had happened. He looked down at the floor.

Jan sat very still, considered how to respond. "Uh huh. You had a feeling something was wrong. Go on."

"Yes, it was like the girl was drugged or something. Later she ended up in a canal in Amsterdam, dead."

"Hmm. Well, I'm glad you reported this to me. Did you check the paperwork?"

"Yes, of course."

"And the I D ? "

"It matched."

"Good. Then it's all clear on our end. You did your job and that's all you should worry about." Jan relaxed back into his chair, with a slight hint of a smile.

Stunned, Rob looked up, wide-eyed. "But they used me to get the girl through customs smoothly."

"I just asked if her paperwork was in order." The slightest bit of annoyance crept into Jan's voice.

"And it was. But maybe it was a fake passport."

"Was it?" Jan was still sitting back in his chair, but any trace of a smile had vanished.

"I don't know. It looked okay."

"If customs thought she was okay, it's not your problem. We're clear on this end." Jan's voice held authority and conviction. He sat upright in his chair, back ramrod straight.

"But--"

"I believe your shift has started. I'm sure the police will handle this. Thank you for bringing this to my attention, though."

Jan turned to pick up the phone and Rob saw that he was dismissed. He got up and left the office without another word. He wasn't just stunned, he was angry. Clearly Jan was not at all concerned that a child, whom Rob had escorted just yesterday, had died. Apparently, his only concern was that Rob had followed the rules, that the paperwork was in order, and that the company could not be blamed in any way. What was the matter with him? A child had died!

How many unaccompanied minors had he picked up over the last couple of years? Hundreds? He'd never thought much about them. He'd perused their paperwork as he'd been trained to do, and helped them through customs and passport control. He always checked to make sure the person picking them up had some sort of ID that matched the name that was given to him on the transport paperwork, but it could be anyone, under any name. Until now, he had never given those kids another thought.

But none had ever affected him the way Naima had, even before she had met such a tragic end. He had only done his job. What more was he even allowed to do? And yes, the useless paperwork was all in order. So why was he so angry with Jan?

Rob needed to find someone who understood his concern, who would know what action he might reasonably take. In between rote pickups and drop-offs, he made his way to the airport security office. Someone he knew, at least in passing, worked there. Surely a security officer would take him seriously and have some idea about what to do.

He spotted his acquaintance almost as soon as he entered the office. Ko did not fit the stereotype of the taciturn, straight-faced security officer. Rather, he was slightly pudgy and friendly-looking. He smiled immediately as he recognized Rob and came over to join him.

"Hi, Ko, can we talk for a minute?"

"I'm just on my way to get something to eat – can we walk and talk?" Ko unconsciously touched his belly as it growled.

"No problem." Rob would have preferred to stay in the relative sanctuary of the office, but he knew Ko worked on a strict schedule and one couldn't easily interrupt his short meal break.

They left the colorless security office and wended their way into the public shopping and eating concourse. An explosion of bright signs and cheery holiday displays buffered the din only slightly. The airport was crowded, and the noise was almost overwhelming. Nonetheless, Rob persisted. "Did you see today's paper?"

Ko nodded distractedly.

"I know the girl who was found dead in the canal. She was my pick-up here."

"That's too bad. I'm sorry," Ko said, as if by rote.

A lost traveler waving an airport map button-holed Rob. "Excuse me, could you tell me where the arrivals hall is?"

Ever the courteous airport employee, Rob took out a pen, marked the route the traveler needed to follow, and handed it back with a brief explanation.

As he and Ko resumed their walk, Ko asked, "Are you sure the girl in the paper was the same one?"

"I am absolutely sure!" They were interrupted by another traveler, this one looking for directions to the duty-free shops. Once the man had scurried off, Rob asked, "Can you do something?"

"Do something? Like what?" Ko inhaled the mouth-watering scents from the closest grouping of eateries.

"I don't know. File a report? Contact the city police?" Rob could see, as Ko waved a greeting to another Airport Security Officer, that he, like Jan, really did not want to get caught up in Rob's drama. But Rob was resolute. "Ko!"

"Yes, I'm listening." He was, but only just. There was a lunch specials menu offering a good deal on a *kroket* and *frites*, with a large drink.

"The people who picked up the girl just did not seem right to me. They gave me a bad feeling."

"I'm sure you must be mistaken. Did you verify ID?"

"Yes, of course."

"That's all you can do."

Undeterred, Rob stubbornly continued, "What about you?"

"Look, Rob, I'd love to be able to help you, but did you see a crime happen here in the airport?" Ko's stomach growled again.

"I--no. It was just like I said, a bad feeling."

"You can't do anything about that. And I really cannot do anything about that either. My jurisdiction is only here at the airport." Seeing Rob's face fall, Ko continued hurriedly, "Hey, it's okay: you did the right thing. If you feel like you know something useful about what happened, you should talk to the city police. And in the future, if you see a crime occur inside the airport, come to me."

Dejected and frustrated, Rob thanked him, turned on his heel and walked away. He went back to continue his shift.

As he picked up his assigned passengers, he appeared to be his normal, composed self. Below the surface, though, he was seething with righteous indignation. He just could not let it go. A little girl had died. Since no one at the airport seemed to care, first thing tomorrow morning he would go to the police station closest to his apartment. He was pretty sure they weren't as corrupt as he had heard they were in some other countries, but he hadn't had any personal experience with the police and wasn't sure they would take him seriously either.

Before he left the airport, he made sure he had made a copy of Naima's transport paperwork. Those records weren't kept long term, but rather the paperwork was put into temporary storage before it was destroyed. Nor was there a database kept to look up U.M. information later. In fact, anyone could drop off a child at one airport, and anyone could pick up the child at another. No one ever asked what the child's final destination would be, much less verified an address. By using the U.M. services, the unaccompanied minor could avoid the usual customs lines and scrutiny. It was so streamlined that the airport had recently broadened the services to include assistance for VIPs, so they could also go straight through customs and security without a long wait with everyone else.

As Rob rode the train home, he dredged through his memory, trying to remember the U.M.s he had escorted over the years. Most were rich kids, usually children of diplomats or international corporation executives, nothing like Naima. Some were demanding, spoiled brats; some were just cranky, tired little kids being shuffled between divorced parents; while others were sweetly polite or excited. He could not recall any youngster who was totally silent like Naima or who, in retrospect, seemed as terrified as she had been. The more he thought about it, the guiltier he felt.

Lost in speculation, Rob nearly missed his stop. He'd best put these thoughts aside and get himself together.

He walked briskly the few blocks to his apartment, cooked and ate his usual simple supper, and washed up the dishes. Once again, routine helped to settle him down. He carefully avoided looking at the picture of the dead girl as he placed the newspaper into a drawer and closed it decisively. He attempted to read a few chapters of a book before turning in and sleeping a dreamless night.

Rob anxiously entered the local police station first thing in the morning. It was larger than he had anticipated, and efficient-looking. He approached a uniformed cop at the main desk and blurted out, "I have information about the dead girl found in the canal."

"Do you have an appointment?" was the reply. The officer barely looked up at him, and never stopped typing something into a computer.

"Um, no."

"Take a number, fill in this form and return it to me. After that, we can assign an officer to take your statement."

Rob accepted an Incident Report form and a pen the cop handed him, grabbed a number and sat down to complete the form. When he was done, he returned the form to the cop at the information desk and settled in to wait.

Sometime later, another cop showed Rob to a small interview room containing only a table and two chairs. He felt uneasy, as if he was a criminal being taken into interrogation, but he sat and waited quietly.

Finally, a plainclothes officer entered the room and introduced himself as Officer Brandy. Rob noticed with dismay that the officer was out of shape, wore wrinkled clothing, and looked to be approaching retirement age. In addition to Rob's completed Incident Report, Officer Brandy carried a pad of paper and a pen.

"Would you like something to drink? Coffee?" It was a polite offer, but the tone was uninterested.

"No, thank you." Rob's mouth was dry, but he was antsy and didn't want to wait anymore.

"Did they get all your personal info at the front?"

"Yes, and it's on the form as well." Rob's heart sank as he saw that Officer Brandy seemed surprised both that he had the form in his hands and that it had Rob's personal information on it.

The officer plopped down in the chair across from Rob, scanned through the form and said, "Yes...Why don't you start at the beginning? I'll let you know if I need any further details."

With a faint glimmer of hope, Rob began a rushed explanation. "I work at the airport. I'm a Passenger Assistant, escorting unaccompanied minors, elderly and disabled people - anyone who requires assistance - through the airport."

"Yes, I'm familiar with that service. I've used it myself. In fact, there's a lovely young lady who helped me last time. Gina, I think was her name. Do you know her?"

Trying not to look as annoyed as he felt, Rob said, "No, I'm sorry I don't."

"Maybe it was Janeen. I'm not as good with names anymore." His gaze drifted away, with the slightest of smiles curling his lips.

"About my report..."

Officer Brandy pulled his focus back. "Oh, yes. I see you might have information about the girl in the canal - you think she came through the airport?"

"Yes." Rob did his best to keep the rising impatience out of his voice.

"We're still trying to figure out who she is - no one reported a missing person."

"Here is a copy of the service request form. The names are also written in my report."

"Ah. I see it. Can you expand on the 'bad feeling' mentioned here?"

"When I first picked up the girl, it was really busy. She was quiet; I don't think she said one word--"

"She was coming in from India? Perhaps she couldn't understand English?" Officer Brandy continued to scan through the form, bemused, not really looking at Rob.

Stubbornly, Rob continued, "The girl wasn't dressed for the weather, no coat or winter boots and no luggage. I spoke with the woman who picked her up, who said she was her sister."

"And she spoke English?"

"I think she was English, British."

"Used to be a colony, India."

Barely able to contain his impatience, Rob snapped, "Yes, I know."

"Did you verify the sister's I D ? "

For what felt like the hundredth time, Rob affirmed that he had. "Yes. It matched the name on the U.M. paperwork, which you have a copy of there."

"I see. Go on."

"That's it. I read in the paper the next morning that the girl was found dead in the canal, and the sketch was of the unaccompanied minor I picked up, without a doubt."

Taking a patronizing tone, Office Brandy continued, "Did either the girl or her sister report any problems to you? Were you a witness to a criminal act?"

"Well... no. The girl didn't say a word, as I told you. Her sister - the woman who said she was her sister - she didn't look anything like her!"

"Could be a different father, or sometimes siblings just don't look alike."

"But the girl is dead, and I'm sure it's the same one as the girl I transported!"

"Yes, well, we're still investigating. We don't know how the girl ended up in the canal. It could be an accident, perhaps she was on drugs. Tragic."

"The paper said she might have been killed!" Rob felt like leaping from his chair.

"Oh? The newspaper is ahead of the Medical Investigator's report."

"But--"

Officer Brandy finally looked directly at Rob and took a tone of command, "Sir, if there was a crime committed in my jurisdiction, I assure you I will investigate to the fullest of my ability. If you have information a crime was committed in the airport, please make a report to the airport police."

"I did. I tried to. They said to come to you."

Officer Brandy spoke a bit faster, with a tone of finality, "Thank you for doing that. We'll look into the name you gave us, that might be helpful. When we get the medical report back, we'll know more. I'm sorry." He shuffled the forms and gathered himself to leave.

"I'm trying to explain that this might not be an accident--"

"You've been helpful. Thank you for coming, sir."

As Office Brandy stood up and reached out to shake hands, Rob knew that his visit had been a waste of time. His boss, airport security and now the regular city police were not going to do much of anything about the death of a kid from India. Their indifference was appalling and frustrating. All of them seemed to not want to be bothered; the problem was someone else's.

If Jan or Ko or Officer Brandy had shown any interest in finding out what had happened to Naima, at least some of the guilt Rob was feeling might have been lessened. But he wasn't sure what exactly he thought they should have done either. These guys were supposed to investigate, find out the whole story, hold someone to account for something. But who and how? He was sure no one would tell him if the dead girl was confirmed to be Naima. Nor would they share with him the results of the medical examiner's report. It was all too convoluted. You couldn't accuse someone just because you had a gut feeling, there had to be evidence.

He knew something was wrong, but not what, and he was stuck with that.

Rob tried to keep his emotional state off of his face. He stood up and shook Officer Brandy's hand as civilly as he could muster. He even managed to mumble a fairly polite "Good luck" which got him another curt "Thanks." He left without another word. He simply could not get the image of Naima, of the fear in her eyes as she saw that woman, out of his mind.

Officer Brandy waited until he was certain Rob had left the station before taking the paperwork to his superior, Chief Steunenberg. Officer Brandy's lax demeanor disappeared as he shut the door to his boss' office and quietly showed him the paperwork. "Someone just came in to help identify the girl in the canal."

Chief Steunenberg was a few years younger, but the two police agents were close. They had followed different paths through the police bureau, though. Officer Brandy wanted to stay out working a beat until his age and declining health had forced him to be assigned to desk duty. The chief was more politically motivated and had moved up the chain of command quickly, making friends in high places. He knew how to work the limited police budget, making deals that he felt would best benefit his staff and the public. Unlike Officer Brandy, he had spent very little time out in the field, preferring the machinations of running a bureau.

Both the men were third generation officers and their families regularly socialized outside of work. With more practical on-the-ground experience, the chief trusted Officer Brandy to advise and implement any agreed-upon course of action without question. In turn, Officer Brandy now had a token supervisory position and he didn't have to schmooze with any politicians or bigwigs - something he absolutely despised.

The chief gathered the paperwork from officer Brandy, and swept it into a cardboard box. "What country?"

Officer Brandy sighed. "Allegedly India. We have a name and the date she entered the country. I could search customs."

"Don't bother. They aren't going to pay to get her body back and it's unlikely she's under her real name, given the situation." The chief didn't elaborate, nor did

Officer Brandy ask him to. "Since the press already has the story, just make sure they don't get any more. Get the M.E.s report personally, if you have to. I only want to know if it's ruled a homicide. Either way, keep this between us."

In an uncharacteristic moment, Officer Brandy seemed to be about to retort. Chief Steunenberg stood up from his desk, dropping his friendly and relaxed attitude. "I won't remind you, Brandy, how close you are to retirement. Let's not start some big hassle at this stage."

The police department had sometimes agreed to look the other way when it came to non-Dutch or underage sex workers if it might cause a scandal. They knew who owned and ran the sex clubs and brothels legally, and also knew that there were illegal operations. They were aware that some of the higher-ups who patronized these establishments were the same politicians and VIPs who held both power and money, and could directly affect police budgets. Occasionally there was a cover-up when it was felt that the public needed to keep faith in their government or feel safe in their neighborhoods, and the crime wasn't grievous to the public at large.

There was more emphasis put on crimes where there was a clear victim, or where the broader public might be affected more directly. Nowadays, children were being recruited by terrorist organizations, enticed out of their home countries, trained in the jihadi camps and returned to carry out suicide bombings in public hubs. Money and manpower were both limited, and the police needed to prioritize which cases were more important and how much time one could spend on each. Even knowing that, Officer Brandy still felt conflicted. But the chief was right, there was nothing to gain right now by starting a fuss.

Earlier in his career Officer Brandy had learned that reality did not always match the idealized version of events he had imagined before he became a police officer. He wanted to be the good guy who got to save and protect, like his father and grandfather before him. But the victims he had rescued weren't always appreciative of his help. He once had spent weeks tracking down a missing girl, a teen suspected of running away or being kidnapped by a loverboy. During what he thought would be a rescue, the girl spat and clawed at him as he explained that he was going to return her to her home. And there was no happy family reunion. He had thought he'd be seen as a hero; instead the girl's parents berated him for not punishing her with jail time or teaching her a lesson with interrogation or worse. He still had a small scar where the girl's nails had dug deep as he had physically dragged her kicking and screaming back into the family home. She hadn't left home against her will and her parents didn't really want her back. In fact, it was a neighbor who had contacted the police to begin with. Officer Brandy had followed the law, but in the end, the girl had ended up in a mental care facility and her parents moved to another city.

He had other memories where the lines were blurred between victims and perpetrators, good guys and bad. He had started drinking, at first to relax and come down from the adrenaline high the more intense shifts would bring. Then it got out of control when he was drinking to forget the endless wave of crimes and bad people as injuries and old age began to diminish his effectiveness on the streets. He was beholden to the chief, who had quietly forced him to get help for his drinking, and allowed him to finish out his service with his reputation intact. Even though he had been more than a year sober he still found it difficult to remain on the job without a little something to relax with after work.

He supposed that men in other high-pressure jobs had their own vices, as he had. No matter how many criminals he had taken off the street, there was a never-ending supply of new ones to take their place. There would always be crime, and the world was rarely black-and-white. He had done the best he could do with his career, and it was almost over.

That thought and the years of working at a job that had slowly worn him down caused him to choke back any protests he might have had. He just got up, nodded acquiescence to Chief Steunenberg and left his office. Only a few more weeks and he could shut this chapter of his life completely out of his mind, forever.

# Chapter Three

The walk from the police station back to his apartment helped to calm Rob down, but inside he still seethed. He didn't pay attention to the characteristic row homes flanking narrow canals, and automatically wove his way around pedestrians and bicycles, and crossed cobble-stoned streets traversed by trams, taxis and delivery trucks, with hardly a glance. He was conditioned to the chaos and traffic, and his thoughts were as gloomy as the gray skies above him.

He had always believed that the system, whether corporate or governmental, was reasonably fair. Oh, maybe they were not particularly caring, but he had never imagined they would be so blasé about the death of a child. Sure, he'd suffered at the hands of a court system that favored women in divorce and custody proceedings, but nothing like this. The passing memory of his own divorce had his bile rising and it left a bitter taste in his mouth.

However, even in Amsterdam, the largest city in the Netherlands, there seemed to be relatively few major crimes. At least he had never been touched by it. There were those who pick-pocketed the tourists or stole bicycles, but murders were rare outside of gang on gang violence. Murders of children were rarer still. Regular civilians could not own guns, only the police were allowed to carry weapons. The Dutch were generally tolerant and down-to-earth, a pragmatic people not used to the extremes seen in some other countries where mass shootings, bombings, acts of terrorism and the like were more frequent.

Despite all that, Rob was certain this was something more than just an accidental death. Unfortunately, that was only a gut feeling, and he had no evidence of...well, anything. But he did have an inkling of what might be going on.

He didn't live that close to the red light district or its sex clubs, but he was aware of them. Most were licensed and regulated, with prostitution being legal for those aged eighteen or older. He accepted the red light district as a reasonable response to the human condition. He condemned neither the men who frequented that area nor the women who provided services. Actually, he'd never given it much thought at all.

Now it was beginning to dawn on him that there might be a very dark side to this business right here in Amsterdam. He'd heard whispers about private clubs where illegal things went on, but never really paid attention, assuming they must be rumors about someplace else.

Without thinking about it, he just associated child trafficking with third world countries. Certainly he was aware of the high-end sex scandals with politicians, celebrities and religious leaders being linked to underage boys and girls, but usually that occurred in other countries, not here.

One minute he was certain he had stumbled onto something, and the next he doubted his gut feeling. Was it possible that children as young as his precious daughter, Maaike, could be victims of this horrific abuse, right here? The pieces were seemed to fit together - a little kid, scared to death and possibly drugged had arrived in a winter storm without proper clothing or luggage and he, Rob, had turned her over to that sordid woman and her shady companion. He'd followed the rules. How could he possibly have imagined that the kid would end up nameless and unmissed, her life snuffed out in an icy canal?

By the time he got back to his apartment, the feelings of guilt and outrage were simply intolerable. So Rob did what he always did when faced with difficult emotions. He turned on the TV to distract himself. When that didn't seem to work very well he went to the gym to work out. Before long it was time to go home, fix some dinner and go to bed.

When he arrived at the airport the next morning, Rob appeared to be his usual calm, buttoned-down self. Perhaps he was a bit more taciturn than usual, but you would have had to know him pretty well to have noticed. He picked up his schedule at the Passenger Assistants Office and drove his cart to the first assigned gate to wait for his pick-up.

As Rob was waiting at the gate, Samir happened by and greeted him cheerfully. "Hey, man."

Samir had a beguiling smile. He was naturally thin, taller than Rob, and blessed with exotic good looks. His easy-going nature and innate charm made him an excellent passenger assistant. While he was famous for setting up love connections for other staff at the airport, he was careful to keep his own dating adventures outside of work, which kept him in good stead with the bosses.

"Doing a double, are you?" Rob sometimes envied Sam's youth and carefree attitude, but he was truly grateful. Samir had pulled him through some dark times and had always been there when he really needed someone. Still, Rob's question came out sounding almost accusatory to his ears.

"I'm going to take a break, maybe next week. What's up with you, man?"

Sounding a bit more annoyed than he intended, Rob replied, "I'm fine. What do you mean?"

Samir put on a reassuring smile. "I'm your friend and I can tell something's off since that U.M. Just focus on your job. Pick them up, drop them off. That's it."

Rob's plane had arrived so he checked his PDA again and said curtly, "That's what I'm doing." Maybe Sam was right. He'd developed better composure since the divorce, at least on the outside. It was unlike him now to feel so uncertain and unclear about things and he was embarrassed that it showed. If he returned to his normal routine, he was hopeful that he could regain control over his emotions, at least enough to be able to hide his weaknesses away from the rest of the world.

"I'm here if you need anything."

Putting aside his annoyance, Rob said more pleasantly, "I know, Sam. I'm fine, really, just a little busy. We'll talk later, maybe after work."

Samir, bless him, just gave him a big grin and dropped the subject, taking him at his word.

The rest of the day passed swiftly, with one pick up after another. Most were elderly folks who just needed assistance to navigate the large, busy airport. Rob managed to project a pleasant, if somewhat reserved, front. He always took good care of his clients.

By the end of his shift, he was feeling more competent and even satisfied with himself as he wended his way through the service workers' hall on his way to the train. He'd forgotten about his suggestion to Samir that they talk after work.

But then from behind, Samir hailed him, "Hey man, hold up!"

Rob didn't feel like talking, he just wanted to get home. Trying to keep his voice neutral, Rob answered, "I've got to catch my train."

Samir ignored the hint as he caught up, slightly out of breath. "You know this place, always the gossip. I heard you went to the police."

Rob raised an eyebrow, wondering who on Earth could have found that out. "That's right. They weren't very helpful."

"You'd risk your job over... what happened, exactly?"

In one breath, Rob blurted out "You know, I told you. I had a bad feeling when I dropped off that U.M. and then there was that article in the paper, the dead girl found in the canal - and the artist's sketch was definitely the same girl I transported. And before you ask, yes, I checked the ID. The paperwork was good. I reported what I knew. I did everything I was supposed to do. Now that's it. End of story!"

Samir would not be deterred. "I'm just trying to be your friend, man. Sometimes you get so emotional over things you have no control over. I'm only looking out for you."

"I know you mean well, Sam, but we've been through all this before especially when you were on me after Carly and the kids left."

"You needed that, man. You were not yourself."

Rob had to acknowledge that Samir had been a good friend during those painful months when he was adjusting to losing his wife and kids. He had barely managed to keep his head above water. First Samir had cajoled him into working at the airport, which had proven to be almost therapeutic. Later Samir had helped by sometimes just listening, sometimes trying to distract him with introductions to attractive women or by diverting his attention with endless invitations to nightclubs. Rob wasn't really interested, but the constant cheeriness of the younger man had been a great comfort.

Samir suddenly clapped Rob on the shoulder and said, "That reminds me. One moment. Wait here!"

Before Rob could voice a protest Samir darted over to a group of flight attendants and brought one of them back over to meet him. Rob had a couple of seconds to observe and he stared, mesmerized. The woman now accompanying Samir was petite, well-groomed, and walked with a gentle grace. Her light brown hair was pulled neatly in a chignon, and her makeup was flawlessly applied. She was a bit older than her colleagues, but seemed quite self-assured with her direct gaze and elegant posture. There was something reserved in her sophistication which made her seem cool at first glance. "Rob, this is Claire."

Feeling trapped and very uncomfortable, Rob pasted a smile on his face and extended his hand.

As they shook hands, Claire said, "We have actually met before, only in passing, though. I fill in as a gate agent quite often." Her voice was soft and inviting, with a noticeable French accent. Her gaze held his and Rob caught the faint scent of lavender. For a moment his mind was transported into the memory of a happy childhood holiday in Provence.

Unnerved, Rob held onto her hand just a bit too long. "Oh? I'm sorry, I don't remember. Nice to meet you again, then." He felt like an awkward schoolboy. This woman reminded him that he had been happy and carefree once, and her warm hand seemed to give hope that those times could come again.

He shook his head slightly to come back to reality. What was Samir up to? It was all rather disquieting, and he threw his friend a desperate glance.

Samir was grinning from ear to ear. "I thought maybe you could talk with her about what happened."

Taking the cue, Claire jumped in, "I heard about your concern for that girl. That is very kind of you."

Rob absolutely did not want to discuss what had happened to Naima, or his failure to do something about it. It had consumed his mind for most of the day. Without thinking he stiffened and pulled away, all the good memories dispelled. The gossip mill had apparently been working overtime. He hated how news got around the airport so quickly, and was unsettled to think someone had seen him at the police station. "It doesn't matter. I told the police what I know. It's up to them now."

Endeavoring to hold his attention, Claire tried her best. "But they will do nothing. I know a few people, I could give you a lift into town and possibly--"

"Thank you for the offer, but I can't right now."

"This is a problem that may come up again. When you have the time--"

"I apologize. I must get my train. Good evening." With that, Rob walked stiffly away without a backward glance. It was all he could do to keep his swirling emotions in check. He was attracted to Claire, more so than to any woman in many years. That attraction was all mixed up with his feelings of guilt and inadequacy about Naima. And then there was the anger and helplessness he felt in the face of the indifference he had encountered. And on top of all that he was going to miss his train!

Claire was surprised by Rob's abrupt departure. She could see he was upset. Had she somehow offended him?

"I'm sorry, he is... I don't know. It's not you. He's a nice guy, usually. You're both people who like to help others, and I thought you might get along."

"It is not a problem. I understand. I must be going as well. Do you need a lift?"

"No, the train is fine. Thank you." They parted; Samir toward the train station and Claire in the direction of the employee's parking lot.

Despite having just worked three flights back to back, Claire still looked immaculate. Her makeup was artfully applied to minimize the faint lines that were beginning to emerge, and to highlight her beautiful blue-grey eyes. Claire was named for her grandmother, who had been a hero of the Resistance during the Second World War. Claire's mother was extraordinarily beautiful and had achieved a certain level of fame as a fashion model back in the day. Her taste in clothes and men was impeccable, and she had expected her daughter to follow suit.

But Claire valued inner gifts more than outer ones and enjoyed reading a good book or taking a class to expand her horizons far more than fancy soirees and fine accouterments. Nor had she ever managed to achieve the perfect figure or flawless features like her mother's. Thus Claire had spent more time with her grandmother and was closer to her. Even after her grandmother's death, she remained somewhat distant from her mother, who, like Claire, kept a busy schedule ahead of her personal life.

Claire had grown up listening to stories of her grandmother's adventures as she extracted secrets from German officers to pass on to her compatriots. Her grandmother had certainly known how to charm a man without compromising herself. Claire had not inherited either her mother's extraordinary beauty or her grandmother's fearless daring. She was attractive enough, and certainly had an adequate fashion sense, but she could not compete with those two women. Neither her father nor grandfather had been present much in her early years, and both had long since passed on. So Claire had learned the most from the women in her life; how to please by being sensitive to others' needs and responding to them. As soon as she turned 18, Claire trained as a flight attendant and she had lived on her own since then. She knew how to serve and also how to keep things cool, whether it was a drunken passenger or a screaming baby. These skills had stood her in good stead as a flight attendant for over twenty-five years now. She enjoyed her job and was very good at it.

Recently though, particularly since the merger of her French airline with its Dutch counterpart, flickers of uncertainty had begun to intrude. Some of her longtime colleagues had taken early retirement, and there were rumors that it had not been entirely voluntary. There were the usual discussions of how old was too old for cabin personnel, and how far the rules could go for weight, height and looks requirements. As with many service businesses, there were guidelines on paper, but behind closed doors, another set of rules could be enforced. The pressures of constantly trying to maintain the correct weight and the subtle ageism on the job were beginning to bother her more and more.

Such were her thoughts as she drove from the airport to the apartment in the suburbs of Amsterdam that she shared with several other flight attendants. Claire's real home was her beautiful apartment in Paris. It was furnished with mementos from her travels, as well as the furniture she had inherited from her grandmother. It was there that she could most be herself, although it was rare for her to be able to spend much time there. Maybe in a couple more years...

Naturally, Rob had missed his direct train. He sat on a bench on the platform, trying to keep warm in the windy train station. Another train should come in a few minutes, but he'd have to change trains in Amsterdam *Centraal*. Or maybe he should switch there to a tram. It was too cold to want to walk, and he was annoyed at having to spend the extra Euros. He was assessing the transportation possibilities when Samir spied him.

"Glad I caught up with you, man. I told Claire all about you, the situation. She wants to help." Samir smiled at Rob's dour countenance.

"Yeah? I don't want to get to know her like this, not now." Rob had no desire to get involved with a woman at this time in his life. He liked to feel in charge of things, in control and he didn't feel that way at the moment. Quite the contrary. He felt as though his world had been turned upside down. A child had died and it seemed there was nothing he could do about it.

Undaunted, Samir persisted, "All's I'm saying is this is a chance to get to know her. She's interested, and maybe she can help you. Or maybe you two can, you know, hook up."

As annoyed as he was, Rob could not help smiling back at Samir's wicked grin. There was something about Sam's cheerful nature and free spirit, that was infectious.

Rob knew that Samir had come to the Netherlands from Yemen as a young boy. His parents had provided a good life for him, and they were financially well-off. They would have preferred that he go to university and become a doctor or lawyer, but that hadn't happened. Their only remaining pressure on their only child was for him to settle down and find a good traditional wife. Still, although he loved his cultural upbringing and his parents, Samir was not ready to give up his current lifestyle, and he would not be coerced. He enjoyed the nightlife, the freedom to travel throughout Europe without too much responsibility, and to mingle with people from many countries and cultures. Samir enjoyed his job at the airport and he was well-known for being as much a playboy as a matchmaker, generous of spirit and kindhearted.

So Rob simply said, "I know you mean well, but--"

With that, Rob's train was announced and his protest was forgotten. They hastily exchanged pleasantries and parted as the train pulled in.

# Chapter Four

Rob enjoyed five blissfully ordinary days. Routine was so soothing. Even the weather had cooperated - cold, sunny days, little wind, and virtually no weather-related flight delays. Rob's assignments had been pretty conventional - mostly elderly folks plus a few young people with skiing injuries and a few unaccompanied minors who were sons or daughters of diplomats traveling to spend the upcoming holidays abroad.

He had gotten pretty good at blocking out thoughts of Naima. His feelings of guilt and outrage had begun to fade into the background, although he was still reminded of her when he read his morning paper. There was no follow-up story, and no one had let him know if it was indeed Naima, or the child's cause of death. He suspected that there were times when a story that might affect tourism would be kept out of the paper. Certainly, a murdered foreigner might be bad for business.

Sometimes that horrifying picture of Naima would appear unbidden once again, but he always managed to erase it as he reminded himself that everyone from Samir to the Amsterdam police had assured him that, since he had followed all the rules, he was not responsible and there was nothing he could do.

But then everything changed, including the weather. The sun was obscured behind an ominously dark sky and strong winds came roaring in from the North Sea, disrupting air traffic and causing major delays.

So it was a scene of barely controlled chaos that greeted Rob that day at the airport. He picked up his list of passenger assists, parked his cart at Gate 9 and awaited the arrival of a flight from Portugal that was carrying the U.M. he was to meet. It was already nearly an hour behind schedule.

Since the flight was so late and he was in danger of missing the next pick-up on his list, he didn't wait until the flow of deplaning passengers had subsided. He barely got a nod from a gate agent as he rushed by, but he knew his ID badge was prominently displayed and his passenger assistant's uniform, immaculate. Ignoring the bustle of irate passengers besieging the airline personnel, he made his way through the throng onto the plane and picked up the U.M. paperwork that was lying unattended on the galley counter. He checked to make sure it matched the information he had, and made his way to seat 15F, where he found a stunning, dark-haired exotic young girl sitting quietly, discreetly observing the action around her.

"Rayna?" He was sure this was she. Nobody else was still in their seat and this was the only youngster still in the cabin.

A broad smile spread across her face as she looked up at him. She had unusually bright hazel eyes, a color he had never seen before. "Yeah, hi."

She had a soft, husky voice with a thick accent. Spanish, maybe? She sounded more South American than Portuguese. He'd heard many accents over the years, but wasn't that good at placing exact geographical locations.

Rayna's hair was a dark chocolate color, worn loose with soft waves. Her skin was a natural tawny shade, and her features seemed sculpted with perfect symmetry, making her almost appear to be a living doll.

Framed by her dark coloring, her eyes were quite striking. They were large and almond-shaped, with irises that were a combination of green and gold, almost as if they were sparkling.

Realizing his mind was going off on a tangent, Rob pasted on his professional smile and extended his hand. "I'm Rob. I'll be taking you through the airport today."

Instead of shaking it, Rayna grasped his hand gently and used it to pull herself up and out of the seat, as lissome as a cat. In her other hand was a little pink backpack with some kind of animal character on the front, and her nails were also painted pink. She was petite and thin, but as lithe as a ballerina. Although she was clearly pre-teen, there was something about how she carried herself that seemed far more... mature.

"Uh, there you go. Come with me."

Much to Rob's consternation, Rayna kept hold of his hand and stuck close to him as he led her down the aisle and by the last of the passengers still retrieving their luggage from the overhead bins. Far from shy, Rayna seemed to enjoy, even relish, the physical contacts that occurred as they wended through the aisle, and he noticed her smiling up at the men they brushed past in a subtly provocative way.

Even as they emerged from the plane and walked towards the cart, Rayna continued to hold Rob's hand. He turned his head slightly to try to assess her without being caught at it.

She was wearing a little denim miniskirt topped by a plain tee-shirt and light jacket. Her attire was very like Naima's, except for her shoes. Instead of sandals, she wore short, flat-soled boots that didn't really provide protection for her bare legs. When he got a really good glance at the pink backpack with its distinctive animal character, he had to take a deep breath to steady his nerves.

At the cart, he gently detached himself from her grasp and said, "You can sit up front here." He kept an eye on her as he moved around to sit in the driver's seat. She smoothly slid her body onto the seat, arranging herself almost as if she was posing. She was like a little movie star, aware of everyone around them and Rob noticed a few gazes in her direction as well.

The memory of Naima flooded Rob's mind as he sat down, of how disconnected and silent she had been, and distracted, he didn't notice how Rayna leaned invitingly towards him, her thick, dark hair falling slightly over her unusual eyes.

Rob banished his memories and silently vowed that whatever happened, this time would be different. He had to be sure though. Concern propelled him to try and make small talk, something he was not supposed to do with clients, but he needed to find out if his fears were founded or not. "So, are you from Portugal?"

"No, not from there."

Her English was good, even with the strong accent. He still couldn't place it. Her voice was soft and sweet, but it had an energy that hinted at something powerful behind it. Like a honey bee with a hidden stinger. She didn't elaborate on her answer, so he tried again. "Okay. Are you here for a visit?"

"Yeah. I visit my sister."

Rob struggled to keep his breathing steady as his foot slipped off the throttle and the cart slowed. He recovered quickly, but was suddenly at odds with the traffic flow in the concourse, and even using great skill he only narrowly avoided several mishaps. "I hope you brought warm clothes."

"I no have any. My sister, she gives me something. Can we stop? I have to go to the toilet, please."

"Sure." he said, relieved that she had provided a diversion. He tried to gather his thoughts - what should he do?

Thinking fast, he guided the cart out of the main airport throngs and into a side hallway in a section of the airport that was mostly closed for renovations. There was no through traffic, and 'under construction' signs in several languages blocked the other end of the corridor. He stopped the cart and indicated the door to a small ladies' room. "Here you are. Take your time."

As Rayna slid out of the cart, Rob got a better look at her backpack. It was identical to the one Naima had been carrying just a few, but very eventful days before. "Uh, Rayna?"

"I come right back, quick," she declared and quickly entered the lady's toilet before he had a chance to say anything more.

As he waited, Rob was assaulted by memories of Naima - the same backpack, no winter clothing, being picked up by a sister who would provide all the necessaries. Uncanny! Could this possibly be a coincidence? Not too likely. Rob's thoughts were swirling between the past and the present. He see-sawed between trusting his gut and doubt - after all, he could be mistaken.

Suddenly he realized quite some time had elapsed and Rayna had not emerged. He checked his PDA, then his watch, then checked them both again. Fortunately, he had chosen well and there was no one else in this side hall. He glanced at the distant wall of windows and saw that snow was now blowing in the fierce winds.

He glanced at his watch pointlessly yet again, and looked around. He didn't know who or what he was looking for in the deserted hallway. Should he call someone? And say what? He shook his head at himself, forced himself to get up and walk over the ladies room door where he knocked tentatively. "Rayna? Are you okay?" When there was no answer after a long moment, he knocked again. "Rayna? Are you okay?" He felt like an idiot, confounded by a little girl and repeating himself.

There was still no answer. He put his ear to the door and heard sounds of what seemed to be muffled sobbing. A crying female had always been a weakness of his. "I'm coming in, okay?"

Gingerly, he opened the door and entered a dingy, narrow restroom. It was empty, except for Rayna curled up in the far corner. She looked up as he entered and he could see tears flowing as she rocked back and forth, arms around her bare knees. He rushed to her. "Hey, are you okay? What's the matter? Are you hurt?"

A faint memory bubbled up in his mind of his daughter Maaike, about age six or seven. She had fallen out of a tree and had fractured her arm, nothing serious. But he had been at work and unable to get away. His ex-wife wasn't really sympathetic, and Maaike had called him from the doctor's office, weeping uncontrollably and looking for comfort. He'd felt like such a cad, and the guilt of not being there in her time of need had lingered.

Rayna's soft voice startled him out of his memory.

"Please..." She looked up at him through thick lashes, her face wet with tears.

He crouched down beside her automatically, thought better of it, got up, retrieved a paper towel, and gave it to her as he crouched down again. "Please what? What's wrong?"

"Please help me." She dabbed the towel on her face, never releasing his gaze. Even in the dim light, the gold flecks in her eyes shimmered.

"I'm trying, but I don't know what's wrong." But his gut was warning him that he did.

"It very bad. You have to help me!" Rayna started crying again in earnest.

Never comfortable around displays of emotion, Rob looked around for someone who might help him out. Of course, there was no one. He sat down fully beside her, unsure of what to do or say.

Rayna threw her arms around his waist and collapsed into his lap, sobbing bitterly. He awkwardly patted her on the head while pulling back as much as he could, now praying no one would come into the restroom. "I'm sure it's not as bad as you think. Why don't you tell me what's wrong and I'll see what I can do to help you."

Rayna sat up and wiped her eyes again. Sniffling, she looked up at him, seemingly unsure or scared, both probably. "They... they wait for me. I no want to go with them, please!"

"What? Who is waiting for you?" He wanted to know, and yet he didn't.

Rayna rummaged in her backpack, retrieved a piece of paper with a blurry, faxed picture and thrust it at Rob. "I'm gunna be picked up by them."

Although the picture was of poor quality, Rob instantly recognized the swarthy man and fat woman from a few days earlier and mumbled, "I've seen them before." Any faint hope that he might be mistaken about this situation was dashed.

He studied Rayna's sad face for a moment and then said flatly, "She isn't your sister."

"They tell me to say that."

"Who told you that? Why?"

"To tell you now is too long. They are very bad people. I no want to go with them. Please help me."

Rob sucked a deep breath in. It was not a coincidence. It was Naima all over again. What could he possibly do? Old habits prevailed, "I'll take you to the police."

But Rayna was not the docile, quiet Naima. She jumped up and shouted, "No!" Now he could see the fire in her eyes and hear the anger in her voice. Her posture was stiff and defiant, and not child-like at all.

Afraid she might bolt, Rob immediately stood up too. Even though he knew his words might be untrue, he tried to reassure her, "They can help you."

"No, they can no help me. You no understand. They will only send me back."

"I don't know what to do to help you. You're right; I don't understand what this is all about." That was the most truthful thing he'd said in a long time.

Rayna snatched the fax back and stuffed it into her backpack. "I can no tell you all what I feel. Please... I would more want to kill myself than keep on in life like this, with this lady." She gestured angrily with her backpack.

"Okay, okay. You don't need to do anything like that. I will... I will try to help you."

Rayna sagged, grabbed Rob around the waist and embraced him tightly. "Thank you, thank you."

The soft, sweet tone of an innocent little girl was back, and her helplessness flooded over him. Again feeling very awkward and uncomfortable, Rob just patted her on the head for a moment.

Finally, he came to a decision. He would get her out of here. Then what? No time for that thought: he knew they were already overdue in the arrivals hall.

Adrenaline coursed through him, and common sense left. "Stay here. Don't go anywhere. I'll be back in ten minutes." He pried her off him and took a step toward the door.

"No, please, no leave me. I am afraid." Her eyes were huge, and he saw genuine fear in them.

"It will be okay. I promise to try to help you, but you will have to trust me. Okay?" He didn't know how, but determination gave strength to his words.

Rayna gave him a wide-eyed, wet-lashed glance, hesitated, and then gave him a quick hug. "Okay. Hurry back."

Rob strode decisively out of the restroom, jumped into his cart and drove off at top speed. For once, he was going to be the man he should have been. He would not fail this little girl as he had his own. He had failed Naima too. He squashed his emotions and memories down and hid them with a sudden plan of action. Don't think – move!

As soon as Rob had gone, Rayna's physiognomy changed. Gone was any vestige of uncertainty or innocence. She carefully washed her face, erasing any evidence of tears. She combed her long, dark hair and applied a bit of lip balm to her full lips. In the dim light of the restroom and with her elegant posture she could have been mistaken for a petite woman. When everything appeared perfect, she patiently settled in to wait for Rob's return.

# Chapter Five

It required all of Rob's formidable skill to steer his cart as fast as he could through the swarms of bustling travelers without causing an accident. He headed toward the Air France gates where he hoped Claire was working.

He stopped abruptly when he spotted her, jumped off the cart and hurried past the line of passengers she was checking in. She was picture-perfect, not a hair out of place, and wore a congenial smile that never faltered.

Rob slowed as he reached her, remembered almost too late to calm his breathing and straighten his uniform. "Claire, I must talk with you." His voice betrayed his anxiety, but Claire didn't lose her pace.

Even as she continued to check boarding passes and motion passengers towards the gangway, she responded pleasantly, "Oh, hello Rob. How about lunch?"

Rob responded testily, "No."

Somewhat startled at his lack of decorum, Claire glanced over at Rob but only raised a questioning eyebrow. He managed to pull himself together and tried to backtrack, "I mean, lunch would be great. But I need to ask a favor, now."

Maintaining her usual poise, Claire turned her attention to the next passenger waiting to board, "There you are. You can board now, thank you for your patience. Enjoy your flight." She handed a boarding pass to the passenger who snatched it without a word and hurried down the gangway.

The next passenger in line jostled Rob aside. Undaunted, Claire smiled politely at the man, checked his boarding pass and motioned him on. Without turning her head more than a fraction, she murmured to Rob, "Can it wait?"

"I'm sorry, it can't. It's urgent." He was still breathing unevenly, and Claire glanced up at him sharply.

She studied his face for a moment and then signaled to another gate agent that she wanted to take a break. The other agent nodded assent, waved her off and hurried over to take her place.

Claire said, "All right. Come with me." She led him a short distance to an unused gate where there was some quiet and a bit of privacy. Although there were places to sit, Claire remained standing with no hint of what she might be thinking.

Rob had a brief thought flit across his mind, wondering what his life might have been like if his ex-wife would have been more cool-headed, like Claire. "First, I must apologize for my behavior." He meant it, and hoped that sincerity came through in his voice.

"Apology accepted. Now, you said that you needed a favor."

"Yes, I need to borrow your car."

Both surprised and amused, Claire began to laugh, then saw Rob's face and stopped, "Really?"

"I'm serious. It's an urgent matter."

Although her demeanor remained calm, Claire was taken aback. Here was this man who had seemed rather shy and stiff during their brief encounters suddenly asking to borrow her car. Some nerve! Was he joking? But he did look genuinely distressed and Claire was always ready to help someone in need. On the other hand, she was not about to let a near stranger take her car.

"I can see that you are serious. Look, if we knew each other better, I would be happy to say yes." Rob looked so dejected that she took pity on him, but she was still not willing to let him have her car. So she compromised, "Perhaps I can give you a lift? It is not far that you need to go, is it?"

"I just have to get to my place quickly, by car. It's only about twenty minutes then."

"And when do you need to go?"

Without hesitation, Rob blurted out, "Right away."

Wow, this sounded really serious. Rob must know that it would be difficult to leave in the middle of her shift. Nonetheless, Claire remained her calm cool self as she replied, "This will not be easy. I am filling in for someone else, and this is the middle of my shift."

Embarrassed, yet determined, Rob stammered, "Mine, too. But it's important."

As her natural helpfulness won out over her annoyance and apprehension, Claire said, "I have only another ten minutes required here, then I could switch out the rest of the shift. Fine." Then smiling, she continued, "You are a mysterious one."

Hardly daring to believe his luck, Rob asked, "Yes? You'll help?"

"I will meet you at the departures entrance in fifteen minutes."

Pushing his luck, Rob asked, "Can we meet instead at the side, by the valet drop-off? It is... there is less traffic there."

There was something about this man that she liked, although what it was exactly she couldn't quite place. But she was still smiling when she answered and looking forward to spending the car ride with him. "Okay. Fifteen minutes."

"Yes. Thank you." Gazing into her eyes with relief, he spontaneously grabbed her hand, shook it and held it for a few extra seconds. Then, without another word, he hurried off back to his cart, and she returned to her gate station.

She smiled to herself, amused that she had not minded the lingering touch.

Rob hopped onto his cart and set off at high speed to return to the restroom where he had left Rayna. It took only a few minutes, but he prayed that she was still there, undiscovered by... well, anyone.

He left the cart parked near the end of the corridor, moved quickly toward the restroom door and knocked tentatively. "Rayna, it's me, Rob."

Rayna flung open the door and grabbed him in a tight embrace. He detached her gently. "There's no time. Come on, we have to hurry. I'm getting you out of here. We're taking the back ways, can you be quick and quiet?"

Rayna said nothing, only nodded and shouldered her backpack. They scurried through the hallways and corridors of the airport, wherever possible avoiding the omnipresent cameras in public areas by using service areas and maintenance passages. Rob used his security badge and passcode to get through a couple of side doors. He kept interaction with other personnel to a minimum.

Rayna followed him like a shadow, matched his speed and maneuvers without a sound other than her rapid breathing as she scampered to keep up with his fast pace. Although it seemed like much longer, in about fifteen minutes they emerged onto the tarmac and made their way around the outside of the terminal to the valet drop-off.

Much to Rob's relief, they found Claire waiting in a small, four-door hatchback, car exhaust puffing into the cold air.

Rob yanked open the back door and Rayna slid in quickly. He closed the door behind her and immediately opened the front passenger door and climbed in beside Claire. He slammed the door shut a bit too hard but managed a mumbled apology.

Unfazed, Claire simply asked, "Where to?"

He handed her a slip of paper with his address and asked, "Can we take the scenic route? The weather doesn't look too good for the highway." He seemed nervous and fidgety, which Claire assumed was due to the poor weather.

Claire calmly entered the address into a GPS system, put the little car in gear and remarked, "Not a problem. I did not realize you were bringing a guest. Is this your daughter?"

Rob avoided the question for as long as he could. He pretended to fuss with the seat belts for Rayna and himself.

The little car left the airport and Claire took a scenic route as promised, following a narrow two-lane road alongside what would normally be a picturesque canal. Visibility wasn't too good as it was still snowing and the wind was growing ever stronger, so Claire's attention was centered on her driving. Finally, though, she asked again, "So Rob, is this your daughter?"

Reluctantly, Rob replied, "No, she's not. She's the U.M. I picked up this afternoon."

"What?!" Wide-eyed, Claire slowed the car and pulled off to the side of the road. "Tell me this story from the beginning."

Rob protested, "I don't have time to--"

"We are not going anywhere until you tell me what happened, until this makes sense."

Rob glanced at Rayna, who was cowering in the back seat, clutching her little pink backpack. "I'm trying to help her."

"I have heard that you and I share that quality; we both enjoy helping others. But this is a police matter."

"You know the story, right? I've tried asking them for help, and I was too late to help the other girl."

Turning toward Rob with both frustration and deep concern, Claire replied, "No. I do not mean that. I mean YOU are now the criminal. And you have made ME help in a kidnapping!"

Rob shook his head. "This is hardly a kidnapping. I'm saving her from the real criminals!"

"She is just a child! You must take her to the police so she can be returned home."

Rayna panicked and jumped forward on the seat, declaring, "No! I no have home to go back to!" Only the seatbelt kept her from leaping into the front seat or, worse, jumping out of the car.

Reverting to her flight attendant skills, Claire spoke more soothingly, "We can make sure that you get back to your parents or legal guardian."

Rayna began to tremble in earnest and tears ran down her cheeks. "Listen, miss..."

"Claire."

"Miss Claire. My family sell me into this business. The people coming at your airport, they own me, for debt. They have all my passport papers make for me. If I am returned 'home,' I just go back to work sex, only more worse."

Stunned, Claire replied, "But you are just a child!"

"No, not now. I very old to make much money in my country. I can train the younger ones and also work for some more years here. But I no want that. My family is... no good." Settling back into the seat, Rayna began to share a bit more about her life.

# Chapter Six

Rayna was born in a brothel in Rio. Her mother, Milagro, was just fifteen. Milagro had lived in the brothel since she was twelve. Before that, she had been in brothels in Caracas, Madrid, and Lisbon. Her life as a prostitute had started at the age of five, when her mother, Rayna's grandmother, had sold her to a trafficker.

Milagro thought she had hit the jackpot when Juan, a logistics manager for a healthcare center, decided he did not want to share her with anyone else and lured her out of the brothel. He ensconced her in a nice furnished apartment in a quiet, residential section of Rio. Milagro insisted that there be a room for Rayna, who was then her bright, beautiful and lively two-year-old, and Juan readily agreed. Juan would visit whenever he could get away from his work and family, and Rayna remembered that each time he would bring candy or a small gift.

Later, a baby boy, Ernesto, became a welcome addition. Juan brought new books and toys to keep the children occupied while he visited with Milagro. Sometimes he would take them all out to a local park and they would share popcorn or enjoy a picnic together. Those were the most treasured memories Rayna had, and the only times she had ever felt truly happy. Milagro, who could be quite difficult, was always on her best behavior when Juan was visiting, and she made sure the apartment remained spotless and the children clean and well-presented.

Rayna took good care of Ernesto, and could keep him happy and quiet for hours on end by pretending to read to him from the books. She never really learned to read, but made up stories that went along with all the colorful pictures. Ernesto would laugh or gasp wide-eyed as she acted out mythological adventures of princes and princesses, battles and adventures.

The good life lasted three years and came to an abrupt halt when Juan suffered a heart attack and died. There was a minor scandal when Juan's wife discovered that he had kept a mistress, and Milagro and the children were immediately evicted from the apartment with only what Milagro could carry in a single suitcase.

Milagro had secretly put aside some of the household money Juan had provided and so was able to find a room for rent just outside the slums. Since she had not acquired any other skills, Milagro made a living for her family working the streets in Rio. At age six, Rayna took on the full-time roles of baby sitter and housekeeper. She kept their home neat and at least fairly clean. She did most of the cooking and became the primary caretaker of little Ernesto while their mother was out for nights and sometimes days as well.

Rayna missed the lifestyle they had enjoyed, but made the best of what she had now. She didn't mind her mother's frequent absences, as Milagro always seemed to be irritated, and no longer bothered to help with the cleaning or chores when she was around. Rayna didn't have any books and toys, but she could still make up fantastical tales to entertain her beloved brother.

Milagro became pregnant again and soon found it difficult to find customers. Her meager stash of savings rapidly dwindled. She could no longer pay rent and was once again evicted. They had to move to the slums - the favela - and into a one-room shanty.

Rayna was devastated, but never let it show. She had loved her life with Juan, but what could she do? Although she was wise beyond her years, she was not yet eight years old, and had very little power.

The twins, Luna and Luiz, were born shortly after they moved into the favela. Rayna cared for them too, but she was always closest to her brother, Ernesto. With the twins, there was even less food to go around, and Rayna's chores were doubled as she now had to watch the three youngest while Milagro spent her days and evenings back on the streets competing for what business she could get.

When Milagro became pregnant yet again, Rayna had an ominous feeling. All four children were often hungry, and it seemed there was no chance of them ever going to school, much less having adequate clothing or shoes. Books and toys were nothing but a memory.

It was then that Uncle Teo first entered Rayna's life. Rayna took an instant dislike to him. He was almost as old as Juan had been, but they were as different as two men could be. Juan had been elegant, always beautifully groomed with fancy clothes. He was educated, and spoke well. He had always brought

Rayna and Ernesto gifts on his frequent visits to their apartment, and treated them kindly. Uncle Teo was bowlegged and big-bellied. His clothes were stained, rumpled and ill-fitting. He had a rough voice, and never spoke to the children nor ever even seemed to smile. But there were a few times where he brought over a bag of groceries for Milagro, so Rayna tolerated him.

One day, things seemed different. Milagro was not working that evening, but was wearing the skirt and blouse usually reserved for her nights out. She seemed to be waiting for something a little nervously, and had taken extra care to see that the children were as clean and presentable as possible, given the filthy surroundings. She never explained why, although that in itself was not unusual. Adults generally did not speak to children, unless they were telling them what to do.

Then Uncle Teo dropped by. After what appeared to be a brief but hushed negotiation between Milagro and Uncle Teo, Milagro accepted some money and tucked it into her blouse. Then she called Ernesto to her, gave him a cursory hug and handed him over to Uncle Teo. Just like that. They left together, without even a goodbye.

Rayna never saw Ernesto again. She grieved for him as she did for Juan and the life they had enjoyed briefly, but she was a realist. She knew instinctively not to allow anyone to see her heartbreak. She also developed a way of being invisible to the stream of her mother's dealings with shady characters, and did her best to care for her siblings and to keep them as safe as she could. Rayna knew her best survival strategy was to fade into the background, do what she was told and avoid her mother's increasingly frequent rages. She also figured that, like Ernesto, her days with her family were numbered, once the next new baby arrived.

It had started out as an okay day. Milagro woke Rayna up as she came back from another night out. She had brought back food, and wanted help preparing a meal for the family.

The tiny one-room shanty that they all lived in had no running water or cooking facilities, so Rayna had to fetch a bucket of water while Milagro started a fire in a communal cooking area outside.

Rayna rushed off, looking forward to a good meal, but she dreaded the return journey through the slum. Getting to the nearest water pump was easy, and she could be swift and silent, careful not to bang the empty plastic bucket she carried against anything lest it make a noise and draw the attention of others. Lugging it back after she filled it was difficult; slow and tedious as, even though she was now eight years old, she was small for her age.

Many of the shacks, haphazardly constructed with pieces of wood, tin and other refuse, had no doors. The entrance was often only covered by a blanket or piece of cloth for privacy. People were going about their daily routines in the favela, and even this early the drug dealers and gang members mingled amongst peddlers and hustlers. Rayna's vigilant gaze slid over the hopeless and the forgotten, and kids of all ages, most unattended and left to run wild.

By now Rayna knew how to thread through the maze where there were the fewest eyes to track her, and today she made it back with a full bucket and without any confrontations.

However, Milagro still snapped at her. Rayna had long ago learned to ignore the barbs and occasional physical reprimands, and thus avoided most of her mother's ire. That was just how life was now. Milagro seemed to be eternally pregnant and nearly always in a foul temper.

This time of year the heat and humidity were especially oppressive, and the flies buzzed extra-thick as Rayna stirred a pot of watery stew over the fire. The stench of unwashed people and raw sewage was more pungent than usual in this weather, and there wasn't even the hint of a breeze to bring relief.

Milagro, who would soon deliver her sixth child, held a baby in a sling over her bulging belly as she squatted in the dirt next to the fire, kneading flatbread on a stone. She hadn't been able to work for a while now, and Rayna had a good idea where this meal had come from.

In the distance, the dark skies threatened a summer storm would soon be coming, and Rayna's sense of foreboding grew. The twins were oblivious as usual, 'washing' dishes in a dirty bucket. They often bore the brunt of their mother's acrimony, as she castigated them for the slightest infraction. Somehow, they managed to block it out. It seemed as if they lived in their own world together, a place that only they could see. Sometimes they even communicated with each other in their own made-up language. A bit envious, Rayna sighed to herself, but made certain no one heard.

As thunder growled in the distance, it was no surprise to Rayna when Uncle Teo showed up. Milagro stood up, simpering. "Uncle Teo, welcome. I didn't expect you so early."

Looking at her with disgust, he responded, "What's wrong with you? Can't you keep yourself looking nice?"

"It's not easy since Juan... These ungrateful kids are too much trouble for me."

Uncle Teo's sneer softened, and a mercenary glint sharpened his gaze. "I guess it must be hard for you all alone, without a man. Maybe I can help you."

Despite her condition, Milagro vainly attempted to appear young and sexy. Uncle Teo ignored her and pointed instead to Rayna, "Not you, that one."

Milagro tried to sound plaintive, "She's special. How about one of the others?"

"No." Laughing nastily, his voice became louder and even more grating, "I can't stand the stink in this place. I am only here because of my promise after Juan passed. I have money, you get one less mouth to feed, I choose. That was our agreement. You want to back out, I don't care. I'm leaving." He turned as if to go.

"Wait, I'm sorry." Though her eyes remained hard, Milagro moved suggestively toward him and smiled up at him.

Ignoring the infant swaddled to her, Uncle Teo cupped a sagging breast, assessed it and grunted, "I will come back for you after you clean yourself up."

Lowering her eyes she answered meekly "Yes, thank you Uncle." She accepted a fold of bills he proffered her and concealed them in her blouse.

Uncle Teo turned toward Rayna and spoke to her for the first time. "Girl, come say hello to Uncle."

Although she knew what was in store for her, Rayna kept her face expressionless as she walked over to him.

Indicating the twins, he said, "You want them to have a better life?"

She nodded, trying to take her mind away somewhere, anywhere else.

"Then you listen. You do what I say or they will pay your family debt to me. Understand?"

Once again she only nodded and remained impassive until Uncle Teo ran his wrinkled, dirty fingertips over her full lips. When she involuntarily recoiled from his touch, he smacked her so hard she fell to the ground. "What did I say? Are you deaf or just stupid?"

Rayna got to her feet and stood stock still while that dirty old man touched her, fingered her, disgusted her. Milagro went back to the meal preparation, and no one else paid them any attention.

"You must do better than this to make Uncle happy" he snapped as he grabbed Rayna by the arm and dragged her into the shack. Like the others, it had only a thin, dirty cloth covering the door opening. Since it was a cloudy day outside, it seemed even dingier inside.

No one said anything nor attempted to stop them. Uncle Teo held Rayna down on the floor by her throat. She tried to block out what was happening, begged her mind to go to that place where the twins always seemed to be, far away from the stench and the filth and adults who took pieces of her soul. Tears clouded her vision and the only sounds she could hear were her choking out gasps of air as Uncle Teo's weight pressed down on her, mixed with his guttural grunts.

There was one message Uncle Teo spat out afterward that remained in her memory.

"You learn this good. Uncle will take you to visit many places and give you nice clothes. You are going to a better life, and I will make sure your family gets food and money. Do what I tell you, and none of you will be hungry again. You be bad, I take the little ones instead as payment and leave your slut mother to rot in this stinking pisshole, alone."

And so it was that Rayna left her mother and the only family she had known. She was smart and quickly learned how to curry favor with the men and occasional women who held her life in their hands. She became a master of manipulation. She knew when to be coquettish and when to be the poor little girl, when to smile and when it was safe to sob quietly, alone.

She did her best to put her feelings on hold. She was "good." It wasn't to protect her younger siblings or even her mother. She convinced herself that she didn't care what happened to them. Anyway, she had no way of knowing their fate as she was moved from one brothel or john to another throughout Latin America, and then Europe.

On rare occasions when Rayna did think about Milagro it was with bitterness and anger. She considered her to be weak and incompetent - constantly getting pregnant and having babies. Although she has once been a beautiful young woman, she had not kept herself well, and after the death of Juan, had never been able to do more than work the streets. Life was hard, so maybe it wasn't entirely her fault that her figure was gone along with her youth and beauty.

But the one thing Rayna could not forgive was selling Ernesto to Uncle Teo. The look in her sweet brother's eyes as he was taken away haunted her in her dreams from time to time. She hated reliving the past, but sometimes when she slept the nightmares took over, uninvited. In her mind, she hoped that Ernesto was alive and well, living as a prince in one of the stories she had made up for him so long ago.

Overall, Rayna was a realist; tough-minded, highly manipulative and self-centered, but there was still a part of her that had room for hope, and the faith that things might get better someday. She never forgot the happier days when they had lived with Juan, who in her memories was now embellished as a real prince, far more of a man than he had been in reality. She remembered all the things he had bought her, the pretty dresses and new shoes and the books she had never quite learned how to read. She could still remember the taste of the popcorn in the park, and the smile on Ernesto's face as she shared it with him. So she was, in the back of her mind, always on the lookout for a man who might be her Juan.

# Chapter Seven

Rob, Claire, and Rayna sat in the little hatchback on the side of the snowy road as Rayna related how her mother had sold her to Uncle Teo and into the sex trade. She carefully avoided mentioning any specific locations, dates or last names. Both Claire and Rob were stunned.

"Who is this Uncle Teo?" asked Claire.

Rayna did not answer. She just sat in the back seat and trembled, her eyes wet with tears.

"I think the same couple at the airport are responsible for the death of the other girl - and no one should ever be forced to live a life as these girls have endured. Here: look at her papers."

Rob retrieved Rayna's passport and transfer paperwork from a pocket in his uniform jacket and passed them over to Claire, who scanned them quickly.

Turning toward Rayna, Claire asked, "Rayna, when is your birthday?"

Rayna stared at her blankly, hugged her backpack and sniffled. Finally she said, "It cold here."

Claire turned up the heater, waited a minute or so and then asked, "Where are you from, originally?"

Rayna resolutely maintained her silence, apart from her sniffles.

"I have her origin as Portugal, if her passport is genuine." Rob could still not pinpoint Rayna's accent, and she had been very vague as to locations in her story.

"I see. I have spent some time in that area. The town listed on her documentation is not familiar to me." Claire was also certain that Rayna's accent was not from a European country. It sounded to her like a mishmash of places in South America.

"Not to me either," Rob replied, "And this passport is brand-new."

"You can no send me back to place that no exist!"

"But you are from somewhere..." Claire returned the documents to Rob.

"Where she came from, the people picking her up, they're despicable criminals. They do things like this to children, then they are capable of anything. Claire, please understand. I didn't mean it to happen this way."

"So. We cannot return her to her country or to her family and now the police seem not to be an option as well. Did you have a plan or solution?"

Embarrassed, Rob looked down at his shoes for a long minute and then said, "I didn't think it all through. I missed an opportunity to help before and I won't let the same thing happen again. These are just kids. I'm sorry I involved you in this."

Several minutes passed as Rayna sniffled in the back seat and Rob sat stoically watching the windshield wipers wiping away the snow. Finally, Claire handed

Rayna a tissue, and addressed Rob. "I will take you the rest of the way, but I do not want to be involved in anything else."

"Thank you." There was a maelstrom of emotions in Rob's head; relief, panic, uncertainty, shock. He didn't know what more to say.

Claire pulled back onto the road carefully and continued on towards Rob's apartment in silence. When they arrived, Rob quietly helped Rayna out of the car and hustled her into his apartment building. He was profoundly abashed. He did understand Claire's reluctance to be any further involved, but he was also determined not to allow Rayna to suffer the same fate as Naima had. He felt they were safe for the moment, but hadn't been able to figure out what to do next.

Claire drove on alone to the apartment she shared with other flight personnel. Rayna's brief account of the conditions in which she grew up kept reverberating in her mind. It was truly horrifying.

What kind of woman could sell her children into sex slavery? Rayna had been only eight years old! As heinous as it was, somehow Uncle Teo's behavior was less shocking than the mother's, as she had condoned it.

Although, thank God, she had never been raped, Claire had experienced groping and blatant sexual offers during her years as a flight attendant. There were a lot of dirty old men out there, and it wasn't uncommon to hear about married colleagues hooking up for a bit of fun. Add in alcohol and high altitudes, and things occasionally got a bit out of hand. But as a child, she had lived a safe and well-cared for life and always known that she was loved and cherished. Her grandmother, in particular, had lavished her with affection. Now, as she reflected on her childhood compared to what Rayna had experienced, she realized how privileged she had been. She had never wanted for food; their home had always been beautiful, clean and safe. Survival had not been an issue for her as it had been, and still was, for Rayna.

As sympathetic as she was to Rayna's plight, however, Claire was not going to risk her own livelihood by any further involvement in what amounted to kidnapping. There had to be better ways of dealing with this situation, even if one did not count the police as a solution. Surely she could think of something helpful, if given a little time.

Rob ushered Rayna along the short trek through his apartment complex. He didn't know any of his neighbors well, indeed he had never spoken more than a good morning or good afternoon in passing to any of them. He was aware that this was the first time that he had brought a young child to his home, and that it might be misconstrued. But they saw no one, and he could only hope that no one saw them. Once they were safely in the apartment with the door locked, Rob breathed a sigh of relief. Rayna quickly surveyed her surroundings and continued to shiver despite the warmth. She put down her backpack, looked up at Rob, and wrapped her arms around his waist.

He gave her a moment, then extricated himself from her grasp. He rummaged in a closet, fished out a bath towel, handed it to Rayna and showed her to the bathroom. Still speechless, he indicated the shower and when Rayna began to shed her clothing obediently, he stepped out of the bathroom, closing the door firmly behind him.

In the living room, Rob opened his phone and looked up a business directory online. He began calling the local shelters it listed. He paced as he tried to maintain patience through one disappointing call after another. None of the shelters had any room for one little girl, nor would they accept a foreign minor of uncertain legal status. They kept telling him to take her to the police, who might be able to get her into one of the asylum centers so she could be deported back to her family.

When he contacted the asylum centers they argued that he had to take her first to the police, and it was most likely that, since Portugal is on the list of safe countries of origin, she would be immediately deported. But she hadn't gone through customs and was an illegal, with a passport that that was possibly a forgery, thus Portugal could refuse her return as well. But good luck. Frustrating! He hung up, sat down on the sofa and lowered his head into his hands.

Rayna emerged from the bathroom wrapped only in Rob's short bathrobe. She sat down next to him and tried to cuddle with him. He jumped up and looked around the apartment in the vain hope that there would be an answer as to what to do with this little girl who was acting in such a womanly way.

"What wrong?" she asked.

"I'm trying to find a shelter - someplace that can help you."

"You can help me."

"I've made a lot of calls. No luck so far."

"What wrong with here?"

"I have to go back to work. You can't stay here."

Pouting, Rayna flopped down on the couch and stuck out her full bottom lip.

Rob continued, "You're not just a piece of property, or a stray animal, Rayna. There are rules, laws. I'm trying to do what's right and honestly, at this moment I have no idea what that is."

In the blink of an eye, Rayna switched from sweet, sad little girl to incensed vixen. "You no understand! I have no where else to go, and no one who cares at all for me. I wish I could only die and it will all end!" Having shouted that, she dissolved into tears. She curled into a ball and became the frightened child again. Her sobs were heart-wrenching.

Rob had never been able to stand seeing his daughter cry. He was undone, at a complete loss. Automatically he reacted as he had when his daughter cried. He stepped toward Rayna and was about to take her into his arms when he realized Rayna was not his daughter and was not quite the innocent little girl. He stopped in his tracks and simply murmured softly, "Rayna."

She did not respond. So he tried again, louder, "Rayna! Please. You're right, I don't understand. This is a terrible situation. I had--I have a daughter of my own, just a little older than you."

He moved over to the couch and sat down beside her. He didn't know how to comfort her. He tried to pat her shoulder, then her head. Her hair was damp and it tangled in his fingers. He sensed her innate sexuality and was all too aware that she was naked save for his thin bathrobe, thus his movements were stiff and awkward; mechanical rather than placating. "Okay, listen. I'm doing what I can to find a place for you, people who can help you. But since I haven't been able to find a proper place for you, for tonight, you can stay here and I'll make more phone calls in the morning."

Sensing that it was to her advantage to do so, Rayna remained curled in the corner of the couch and continued sobbing quietly.

"Come on now. It's going to be all right, I promise." He hoped he sounded sufficiently convincing, but in his heart, the uncertainty was crushing and his fear of failing someone else yet again, paralyzing. They stayed together, unmoving, for what seemed like hours. Finally, Rob covered her with his jacket and escaped into his bedroom. He left the door open though, and lay down on top of the bed.

This room was as stark as the rest of the apartment, devoid of color and pictures. Normally he found that to be calming, but at this moment he needed something, anything else outside of this situation to focus on.

The soft sound of Rayna's weeping continued. He sighed, rolled over and reached for his phone. He scoured the Internet, but didn't find any shelters or other resources that he hadn't already called, and it was well after business hours now anyhow.

What could he do? He would just have to leave her here while he went to work and hope he'd be able to make other arrangements for her later tomorrow. Planning ahead really wasn't his strong suit. Well, there was nothing more he could do tonight, so he took his blanket out to Rayna. He retreated back to his bedroom and didn't bother to undress. He lay back down on his bed, set his alarm and drifted into a troubled, uneasy sleep.

To his immense relief, he discovered Rayna was sleeping soundly when he arose and got ready for work. He didn't dare wake her. He left a plate of bread and cheese on the table for her and absconded out into yet another stormy gray day.

He managed to get to work on time despite the weather, checked in, got his schedule and had completed three pick-ups before he had time to pause. He ran into Samir in the break room.

Samir looked concerned, but his tone of voice was less serious than his words. "I can't believe you, man. I agree with Claire, this is a crazy situation for you and for everyone."

"I thought you'd understand, of all people, Sam."

Samir ignored Rob's snappish answer, "What were you thinking? All this time you had the opportunity to hook up with Claire and this is how you get involved?"

Samir's good-natured teasing completely escaped Rob's notice. "That's not it. I told you, I'm not looking for a new relationship. And what was I supposed to do with the girl?"

"Drop her off at the police. Or better yet, don't get involved with that kind of problem at all."

Frustrated, still feeling guilty about Naima, and just a tad self-righteous, Rob replied, "I'm not like that. I can't do that. Not now, not after everything."

"Obviously. Look, man, I know you're trying to help, but let someone else do that."

Rob had accepted Samir's point of view; just be responsible for yourself, and let other people do their jobs. But the people he thought would take care of Rayna hadn't, and he felt trapped. There were so many questions in his head, and he couldn't find a solution for one little girl. He was about to retort when another employee entered the break room. They all nodded hello and Rob waited impatiently until after the employee grabbed a packaged snack and left.

"I have called everyone, and there are no good choices here. So far I haven't found any option at all. She needs a special place where they can address her, uh, issues. Everyone I spoke with simply wants to return her to her country."

"That doesn't sound bad. What about her parents?"

Rob's frustration and confusion were evident and growing as his voice became louder, "Who do you think sold her off into this? I think her passport isn't genuine, and she hasn't been very forthcoming about her country of origin. I already screwed up, so technically, she's not here legally. I don't know what I should have done differently and I haven't figured out yet what to do for her future and safety."

Samir just stared at him, his usual genial smile, gone. "Man, that sucks," he said. "I'd like to help, really, but I don't know what to do either. Where is she now?"

"My place." Rob's answer was more muted, and he didn't look Samir in the eyes.

"What? Alone?"

Rob stared intently at the floor. "Yes."

"Man, you really are crazy! Leaving a kid like that alone, and with this weather, you might not even make it home tonight." Samir checked his phone and continued, "See? The train delays are now up to several hours, and if it keeps up like this they'll stop running."

Rob looked up at Samir sharply as it dawned on him that Samir just might be right about the train situation. His emergency cash was at home, and he didn't have the extra Euros for a rental or a taxi. But maybe if he acted fast, he could avoid having to borrow the money. "I've got some sick leave I can take. I'll try to leave early."

"I doubt they'll let you unless you're dying."

"Talk to Claire for me. Maybe she can give me a lift." In his head, this was a good solution. It also gave him the opportunity to see Claire again. There was something about her... Samir's answer interrupted his musings.

"I'll talk to her, but I wouldn't count on it."

Rob cleared his mind of everything else. "Thanks, Sam." He checked his PDA. The break was over. He left hurriedly and got on his cart, ready for his next pick-up. Just in case Samir's charm didn't work on Claire, he took a moment to utter a quiet prayer.

# Chapter Eight

As she went about her work dealing with tired, irate passengers who were frustrated by the weather delays, Claire kept thinking about her grandmother, that indomitable woman who had risked her life in the Resistance during the Second World War. She had dreamed about her last night. It was so vivid; it was haunting her. True, it was a different time, a time when the lines were clearly drawn, when it was evident who the enemy was. But even then there were many people who stayed on the sidelines, living their lives quietly, only just making ends meet, playing it safe.

What would her grandmother think of Rayna's situation? What would she do? Would she steer clear of Rob, refuse to become any more involved? After all, Rob was kind of a loose cannon, adding on to a situation that was both dangerous and illegal. On the other hand, it was clear that Rayna's life was at risk, and Claire didn't want to see her abandoned into a bureaucratic system or returned to circumstances that were so abhorrent.

The dream had ended with her grandmother standing tall, looking piercingly at her as she declared, "Remember, you are a Fouché. We are intelligent, courageous women of action. We do not look the other way where there is oppression."

So Claire gave some serious thought as to what might be done and who she knew who might be helpful. During her lunch break, she made a couple of phone calls that produced a lead to a special shelter for child trafficking victims in the US. Rayna could stay there and receive professional mental health services.

There were questions about visas and paperwork, but she was certain someone in her network would be able to provide answers. She wasn't sure Rob would welcome the help, but the memory of her grandmother spurred her to action.

As a result, she jumped at the opportunity to give Rob a lift. Samir had called, probably expecting her to refuse but she cut the conversation short by readily agreeing. She chuckled to herself as he hadn't been able to disguise the surprise in his voice.

When she picked up Rob after her shift, she was prepared to gently guide the conversation in the direction she wanted and was looking forward to spending some one-on-one time with him. She drove confidently through the narrow, icy streets, not put off at all by the weather. She was an excellent driver and had had lots of experience driving in similar conditions. She exuded calm.

Not so, Rob. He was very nervous and clutched the door handle, white-knuckled every time the little hatchback seemed to skid or it bounced unexpectedly on the cobbled streets of Amsterdam. He was an expert at driving lower speed vehicles, but less confident with cars or larger vehicles. It wasn't a problem if he was in control and driving, which he had to keep reminding himself that he wasn't. At each perceived slip of the car his foot pressed an imaginary brake pedal.

The weather only added to his nervousness. They rarely closed the roads here, and they were certainly open now, so he had to assume that it was safe. The slightest inclement weather would shut down the trains, though. When the temperature fell to freezing, which didn't happen all that often, planes and trains would be delayed or canceled while roads for cars and bike paths all stayed open.

It wasn't just weather, though, that had Rob so flustered. It was also that he was attracted to Claire and didn't quite know how to deal with that. "Before, I didn't mean to be distant; I just wasn't ready for another relationship. My divorce was pretty bad." He tried to apologize in a calm voice, but it came out sounding a bit shakier than he would have liked.

"I do not go straight from hello, nice to meet you, to marriage. I only want to get to know you better, be helpful and maybe go out, have fun, you know?" She smiled becomingly.

Rob's eyes remained fixed on the road and his voice came out in a bit of a squeak, "Fun?"

"Drinks, dancing, whatever you find fun. I am not looking for a life partner, not now anyway. Just a friend."

"Uh, huh."

Attempting to put him at ease, Claire shifted the conversation. "I am glad Samir caught up with me. I have been thinking about your situation with the girl. I believe I have a contact who might be able to arrange a suitable place for her to stay."

Feeling a bit unmanly and distracted by the stormy elements buffeting the car, Rob responded, "I'm not trying to involve you again."

Claire took her eyes from the road for a couple of seconds to playfully glare over at him. "I am involved again. I am driving the car."

Rob was briefly reassured and captivated by her gaze. He forgot everything for a moment and allowed a smile to ease the tension from his face.

But then the car slipped sideways a bit. Rob's eyes whipped forward and his hand clutched the door handle even tighter. He hoped she hadn't noticed his insecurity.

Claire continued her calm focused driving, but it seemed to Rob that there was mirth hidden behind her words. "I am not sure when I will be free. I am scheduled tomorrow to Brisbane on the red-eye. There are two gate agents out, though, so maybe I can fill in here instead, in case you need me. We could talk again then."

"I'm really sorry about everything." Rob had, at last, managed to suppress the shakiness in his voice.

"I believe you."

As Claire pulled the little hatchback into a space in front of Rob's apartment building, he finally let his grip on the door handle relax a bit, "Would you like to come up? Have a cup of coffee or something?"

Claire peered through the windshield to assess the weather situation. "Sure, that would be lovely."

Rob led them into his apartment building and, key in hand, started towards the door to his apartment and then stopped, listening. There was a pounding beat that seemed to rattle his front door.

Claire asked, "What is that racket?"

Frowning, Rob unlocked the door and preceded Claire into the apartment. As he surveyed his transformed home, his jaw dropped in shock. The stark simplicity he had enjoyed was no more. There were colorful pictures taped on the walls and framed photos of his children on the coffee table. Some type of hideous music blasted from a radio.

And then there was Rayna, oblivious to their arrival, dancing in the kitchen. She too was transformed. She had managed to use some of Rob's clothes to make a sexy wrap top over her mini skirt and had fashioned a pair of his ski socks into thigh-highs. In the middle of a pirouette, she spotted Rob. "Hi!" she called out cheerily.

"What?" was all a stunned Rob could retort, unheard over the blaring music.

Rayna spotted Claire standing behind Rob. Her smile faltered for a second or two, but she recovered quickly. She put down a spoon she had been using, turned down the music, directed a thousand-watt smile at Rob and sang out, "Surprise! I make dinner for you. And I make your house pretty."

"Uh... you didn't have to do all this."

"Is no problem. I want to. You have saved me!" she exclaimed. She ran over and flung her arms around his waist.

At a loss, Rob stood like a statue, glanced over at Claire as if for guidance. She simply shrugged and shook her head.

He gently pried Rayna off. "You said you're making dinner?"

"Oh!" said Rayna and she dashed back to the stove, lifted the lid from a pot and stirred the contents vigorously. The kitchen was surprisingly clean, and the scent of a warm meal wafted through the small apartment.

"It smells delicious." Claire said politely.

Recovering his manners, Rob asked, "Would you like to stay for dinner?"

"I really should be going... the weather is getting worse."

Now the good girl, Rayna responded, "Miss Claire, I make enough. You stay." It was said with a firmness that allowed no argument.

"Well, I... That would be very nice then. Thank you."

As Rayna busied herself fitting three place settings as well as a pot of stew on Rob's little cafe table, Rob turned to Claire, on his best gentlemanly behavior, "May I take your coat?"

"Certainly. Thank you."

He took the coat into the bedroom and returned with a stool.

He informed Rayna, "I don't have another regular chair, I'll use this." He then turned his focus back to Claire, "Can I get you a drink?"

"Just water, that would be lovely."

"Is tap water okay? It's filtered."

"Wonderful, thank you."

He poured glasses of water. There was an awkward silence as they all crowded around the tiny table and Rayna dished stew into the bowls she had set out.

Finally, Rob's curiosity got the better of him. He waved his hand around to indicate the apartment and the meal and blurted out, "Uh, Rayna, where did you get all this?"

"I find the pictures and pretty things in the back of you closet. And the food I get from you kitchen."

"I had meat?"

"You kept your photos in the closet?" Claire glanced around with more interest. The photos were of Rob with a pleasant-looking woman and two kids, a boy and a girl, close in age, at various vacation spots. They showed an age progression from when the kids were babies until they were almost teenagers. Although Rob looked happy in all the photos, his wife appeared less so over the years. The last photo of the kids as preteens was without either parent.

The music still pounded out a beat softly in the background, and Rob couldn't figure out what Rayna had found in his vegetarian kitchen to put into the stew. "This is meat, right?"

He was ignored as Rayna answered Claire's question with eyes wide and innocent. "I find everything in boxes. It look better now, no?"

Rob couldn't help but frown. "There's too much... stuff out here now. My apartment is small; I like to keep it neat."

"Is boring with no color." Rayna was starting to frown and looked a bit pouty.

Laughing, Claire tried a diplomatic interjection. "I agree. Color is good. Are those pictures of your children, Rob?"

"Yes." His reply was curt.

"They are quite photogenic. Do you get to see them often?"

"I, uh, no. Unfortunately my ex-wife, she's... well, I haven't seen them for a while." Hastily changing the subject, Rob directed attention back to the meal. "What is this, Rayna?"

Eating heartily, she responded, "It stew, like I say."

"Really?" Rob couldn't keep the suspicion out of his voice.

Claire chimed in again, "This is quite good."

"I know." purred Rayna smugly.

Rob gave her a mock stern look, and she changed her tone. "Thank you, Miss Claire. I make good wife someday." She gazed suggestively up at Rob through her lashes. He didn't notice. Claire did, but of course, said nothing.

Rayna gave up and turned her attention pointedly to Claire. "Are you marry, Miss Claire?"

"I, uh, no. I am not married."

"Why no?"

Although caught off guard, Claire recovered her composure. "My job keeps me traveling. I do not have a good lifestyle for marriage."

They sat in silence for a few moments while Rob pushed the stew around in his bowl. To distract himself from the mystery therein, he turned his attention back to Claire. "Where do you call home?"

"I have my own apartment in Paris, but I rarely get to see it. With all the traveling, I have come to think of the airline as my home."

"I can understand that."

"I work on a lot of international flights, which is wonderful - I have spent time sightseeing all over the world."

"But not a whole lot of time in your apartment."

He was right about that. Not quite comfortable with the direction of the conversation, Claire laughed and responded, "True. I have been working for... for many years now. I can switch out a shift or two when a gate agent is out, so the work is flexible and stays interesting. I work a lot now so that I can retire early and do something else with my life."

"Like marry?" Rayna wasn't going to let that go.

"I had not given it much thought yet, *chérie*. I would like to do more traveling, but as a tourist."

"I think you life, it sound lonely."

"Well. No. I am fine with things the way they are." Claire was now annoyed that she was being put on the defensive and glanced over at Rob for support. He got the hint and changed the subject.

"Would you like a cup of coffee or something for dessert?"

Rayna got up and automatically started to clear the table.

"No, thank you. I must be going now. The weather... and it is getting late."

"I'll get your coat."

As Rob went for her coat, Claire took the opportunity to address Rayna. "What do you want to do with your life?"

"I want to stay with Rob. Maybe he need a wife."

Claire was amused and was about to laugh when she realized Rayna was not joking. "That cannot happen, *chérie*. He is a grown man and you are, well... you are a young lady who should be in school with a family who cares for you, and friends of your own age."

Rayna glared daggers at Claire and was about to retort when Rob returned with Claire's coat. Rayna quickly erased the frown from her face.

Although Rob sensed the tension between the two women, he had no idea what it was about. "Are you sure about that cup of coffee?"

"Absolutely." With that, Claire snatched her coat, shrugged it on, took a steadying breath, and turned toward Rob. "Thank you. I will let you know when I am back in town. Maybe we can enjoy a cup of coffee then."

"That would be great." Rob barely got the words out as Claire gave a strained smile and a wave goodbye, and let herself out of the apartment without another word.

As soon as Claire was gone, Rayna reverted to the sweet, wide-eyed little girl persona for Rob. "Can we look at TV, please?"

"Sure."

Rayna turned off the music while Rob grabbed the remote and turned on the TV. He sat down on the couch. Rayna hopped up next to him and curled her body against his as he fussed uncomfortably with the remote. He found an old re-run, turned the volume to low, and put his arm around Rayna, who, to his relief, seemed to fall asleep almost instantly.

During the drive back to the shared apartment where she stayed while in Amsterdam, Claire brooded in a feeling of annoyance with both Rayna and Rob. Rayna was such a manipulative vixen on the one hand, and yet she was also just a little girl who was doing what she felt she needed to do to survive. As far as Rob was concerned, she was appalled that he seemed oblivious to the seriousness of the situation and the nature of the attention he was getting from Rayna. Yet he was a good man and his heart was clearly in the right place.

Claire realized she had not followed up on her offer that she might be able to help find a safe place for Rayna. Odd that she had forgotten. She would put her emotional musings aside and continue her efforts to find a more practical home for Rayna, both for the child's sake and for Rob's.

Rob was also brooding as he sat on the couch, not really watching the TV. Rayna's head was on his lap. He was feeling uncomfortable and protective at the same time. After a while, he just wanted to go to bed. Feeling this much guilt and inadequacy constantly was exhausting. Rob gently tried to wake Rayna. He gave her a soft nudge and tried to get out from under her. She just squirmed closer to him as though frightened by something; a bad dream or a memory he supposed. Instead, he grabbed a blanket from the back of the couch to cover them and stayed put.

Rayna stirred, snaked an arm around Rob's waist, then sighed and went back to sleep. He placed his arm over her to comfort her, and against his will, his head drifted back and his eyes closed.

Soon he was also sound asleep with only the white noise of late-night TV in the background. Thus they spent Rayna's second night in Rob's apartment together.

# Chapter Nine

Rob woke up suddenly during the night, startled awake by an unusual noise from the television. It took him a few seconds to realize where he was and that the alarming sound was only something from a commercial.

He found the remote, turned off the TV and noticed he had left the lights on. He managed to extricate himself from Rayna's embrace without waking her and re-covered her with the blanket. As swiftly as he could, he proceeded through his usual nightly routine and settled himself in his bed. He was exhausted. He'd gotten so little rest the night before and he needed to be up soon for his early morning shift. Yet sleep evaded him.

*What was he going to do about Rayna? He could hardly keep her here in his apartment indefinitely. He needed to find a shelter, somewhere safe for her. But he'd called everywhere he could think of without success. Wait. Had Claire mentioned she might know someone who could help? But he had not handled things with her very well, and was loath to admit that he couldn't fix things on his own.*

Fatigue finally prevailed and Rob sank into a fitful slumber. When his alarm startled him in what seemed like only minutes later, he fought himself awake, showered quickly and dressed for work after checking the weather situation - which didn't seem that bad at the moment.

He fixed breakfast for himself and Rayna, and gently woke her. She gave him that big, trusting smile, stretched provocatively and would have wrapped herself around him if he had not stepped back quickly. "Rayna, breakfast is ready. We can eat together and then I have to leave for work. You must stay here today. Don't leave the apartment and do not open the door for any reason."

"I be good. I cook dinner for you. What time you come home?"

"You don't need to do that. I'll pick up something for dinner on my way home. I should be back by four o'clock."

They ate in silence. Rob then got into his coat, checked his pockets for everything he would need at work, and stalled as long as he could. Then he took Rayna by the shoulders, looked into her eyes and said sternly, "Remember, stay here and do not open the door for anyone." She nodded solemnly.

Rayna was attending to the breakfast dishes when he left. He locked the door and felt like he was perhaps indeed a kidnapper, keeping an innocent girl shut secretly in a prison.

As he rode the train to work, Rob berated himself. What had he been thinking? How could he have gotten himself into this situation? What could he have done differently? He could not have allowed Rayna to suffer the same fate as that other little girl, Naima. And now, what was he to do with her? He prayed the answers would come. It should be only a day or two until Claire returned, and maybe he could smooth things over with her then. He wasn't quite ready for her help yet, but he was getting there.

Once at the airport, Rob slipped gratefully into the familiar routine. He had a busy schedule with all the pre-holiday traffic and passengers were more agitated than usual on account of flight delays. It was mid-morning before he spied Samir, who was frantically waving to him. He pulled his cart over out of the main stream of activity to check his PDA and to see what Samir wanted.

"Hey, man. I overheard something. Thought you should know."

"What?" Rob scanned through his PDA.

"Someone is looking for you."

"Who?" Rob was distracted, focused more on the comfort of his schedule.

"I think it has something to do with the girl."

That got Rob's full attention. His head snapped up, schedule forgotten in an instant. "What--no, who's looking? Where did you hear this?

"There's a guy, came into Jan's office. You know I never get involved in other people's business."

Rob sucked in a breath and tried to feign humor to cover his panic, "What are you talking about? You're always interfering in my business!"

Laughing and completely missing Rob's trepidation, Samir responded, "No, man. Just trying to hook you and Claire up. I thought you needed some new--"

"Yeah, okay. What about someone looking for me?" He interrupted.

"I think I've seen the man who was in Jan's office, maybe once or twice before at arrivals. Remember when you had me look up your pick-up info?"

Rob swallowed his rising fear, "Of course."

"It's gotta be the same guy. He's looking for you, or for the girl. Both, probably."

"Do you know that or are you just guessing?"

"Just a guess. The door to the office was closed."

"I'm going home. Can you cover for me? Say I'm still not feeling well from yesterday."

"You're going to lose your job or worse over this. I'll cover for you, man, but I think you're making a mistake. She's still there?"

"It's not like a stray animal I can just drop off at a shelter," bristled Rob.

"There are places here where--"

"Don't you think I've tried all that?" Rob looked around as he realized he had raised his voice beyond an acceptable level. Luckily, no one paid them any attention.

"Whoa, man, I'm just saying--" Samir's tone sounded somewhat defensive.

"It's not that simple, I've been--"

Raising his own voice, Samir interrupted, "Just listen for a minute!"

"Okay, okay. Say what you have to say."

"Don't throw everything away over one girl."

"I'm not. I'm trying to save her--"

"There are probably hundreds more, maybe thousands. Donate your time or money to one of the organizations that help them. Don't do things this way."

Samir's was the voice of reason, and certainly he meant well. Rob knew that. Yet he was too far into this, and now there might be more trouble coming. "Maybe I will, Sam, but Rayna needs someone to help just her and right now. She can't be returned to her country, or that, uh, lifestyle."

"I'm only trying to warn you, man, as your friend."

"Yeah, I know. I just need to figure this out for Rayna. Will you cover for me or not?" Thinking he was about to be called into the boss's office and chewed out, Rob wanted to beat a swift exit.

"I said I would, but--"

"Thanks, Sam." With that, Rob re-started his cart, gunned it and drove off.

Samir shook his head sadly, then walked away in the opposite direction. He simply could not imagine what had happened to his friend. How could he risk his job and maybe even his life for a kid he didn't even know and hadn't even laid eyes on until two days ago?

Rob quickly realized he'd best not attract any attention, so he slowed his cart down, found an inconspicuous place to park it, and then walked as calmly as he could to grab his things and exit the airport. He checked the train schedule on his phone and sighed with relief as he found one departing in just a few minutes. It took all his effort not to run to the platform.

The train ride had never seemed so interminable. He couldn't wait to get home and make sure Rayna was safe, and the flicker of fear rising inside him was close to bursting into flame. With enormous effort, he maintained the appearance of calm while his thoughts had his heart racing. If it was indeed the guy who'd picked up Naima and he was looking for him or Rayna, he knew he was in trouble.

Would Jan have given that man Rob's address? That seemed unlikely, and no one had contacted him during his shift. But even if Jan hadn't given out the address, he'd probably given him Rob's full name. That would be required if the man wanted to file a formal complaint of some kind. It wouldn't have been difficult for the man to track him down after that.

Rob could imagine the interchange between the two men - the swarthy guy being low-key intimidating or affronted and Jan being the calm, in charge customer-service company executive. Jan would have been really annoyed with Rob if the man had come up with a good story. And one would err on the side of the customer. Jan did not like anything that might threaten the reputation of his company or his contract to provide services to the airport. On the other hand, if the man played like he wanted to say something nice, Jan wouldn't hesitate to give out the full name of an employee to someone who wanted to commend their good service. Either way, the man could find out who he was, and it took little effort then to discover his home address. Everything and everyone was registered here with the government. That was another reason why no one wanted to deal with an unregistered, possibly stateless child, who couldn't (or at least shouldn't) be returned to her parent.

Rob hurried from the train station to his apartment. His sense of foreboding grew with each step, with his main concern for Rayna. Please God, let her be safe and help him figure out somewhere else to take her, quickly.

Finally, he reached his apartment door. To his dismay, he discovered it was slightly ajar. The lock had been breached with force.

On high alert, he eased the door open as silently as he could and slipped into his apartment. In shocked silence, he viewed the destruction: furniture up-ended, broken picture glass scattered across the floor, crockery that had shattered when it hit the wall. All signs of a struggle. And he could hear something was still going on in the bathroom. He instinctively moved towards the commotion and his boots crunched on the glass scattered on the floor.

Two burly goons emerged from the bathroom. One was clutching Rayna's arm and he dragged her along as if she were a mere rag doll. Despite her valiant efforts to free herself from his grasp, she was clearly the worse for wear. Her clothing was torn and disheveled and she was breathing raggedly.

When she saw Rob's shocked, white face, she screamed, "Noooooo!"

The thug flung Rayna across the small room. She hit her head on the wall, slumped down and lay still and silent in the corner. The man immediately advanced on Rob who, in his own right, was able to land a couple of good punches before the other thug got behind him and managed to pin his arms. Undaunted, he landed a lucky kick to the groin of the first attacker.

Clearly, though, he was outmatched by these two brutes who proceeded to beat him viciously. Even so, he tried to get to Rayna, whose limp body did not move.

As he was losing consciousness, one of the thugs bent down and whispered in his ear, "Mess with us again and it will be your life. Go to the police, and she will die. Understand?"

They were the last words Rob heard. His final sight was of Rayna crumpled in the corner as the two thugs approached her and the blackness consumed him.

By the time Rob returned to consciousness, daylight had faded to dusk. He came awake slowly, looked around cautiously and realized he was alone. The room was in utter chaos. His body had more aches, pains, and cuts than he could count.

Groaning, he managed to sit up. His clothes were torn and bloodstained. He sat there a couple of minutes trying to collect his thoughts. Rayna was gone. He was profoundly dejected.

But then his propensity for order began to assert itself. He managed to get to his feet and survey the damage.

First things first, though. He limped into his little bathroom. The cuts and bruises on his face were relatively minor, but every breath had him gasping. Before long he had attended to his wounds and even found supportive tape to wind around his torso. Without bothering to get a glass of water, he downed a couple of aspirin before changing into sweat pants and a loose tee-shirt and sweater. It took quite a bit of effort, but he managed.

He knew that once he sat down to rest, he would not get back up to clean up the mess. Maybe once the room was in order again, he could process what had happened and think more clearly - figure out what to do.

So he set to. He swept up the broken glass, and gingerly got the dining chairs and small table up-right again. He put whatever pictures and decorations were salvageable into the closet. Now his apartment looked as if nothing had happened. The only reminder of Rayna was the colorful throw on the back of the couch.

He turned off the lights, sat down on the couch and stared into space. His thoughts were as gloomy as the darkening room; he had failed yet another child, as he had failed his daughter and Naima. He had seriously underestimated the strength and resources of the shadowy people who were now his enemies.

But there was a good chance Rayna was alive and still out there, with them. He wanted to set his mind to figure out what to do next, but fatigue won out. He fell asleep sitting alone on his couch, the thug's warning echoing in his mind. His life or Rayna's if he crossed them...

# Chapter Ten

Claire could not get the beautiful but headstrong child out of her mind. Or Rob either, for that matter. His heart was in the right place, although his methods could use a bit more thought.

Clearly, those two were headed for trouble. And Claire was not looking for trouble. Her foremost goal was to have smooth sailing on the way to retirement within the next few years. What had possessed her to get involved in this situation? Surely it wasn't just that she was mildly attracted to Rob - he was at times so standoffish. He was quite different from the polished, sophisticated men she normally allowed into her life.

And then there was Rayna. Had she been a few years older, Claire might have dismissed her and had little or no sympathy for her. But Rayna was just a child. A child who had been sold into sex slavery by her mother! Claire realized that the manipulative coquettish behavior that so irritated her had probably been necessary for Rayna's survival.

Claire had a soft heart but she was also realistic. She could see that the situation Rob and Rayna were in was untenable and even dangerous. They needed to find a way to get Rayna out of Rob's apartment and into a special shelter as soon as possible. A problem-solver at heart and networker of the first order, Claire mentally ran through the many American contacts she had made over the years.

There were a couple of men she knew in the law enforcement community who might be willing to help. First on her list of leads was Daniel. They had been lovers years ago and had remained friends. Daniel would know what to do.

He was in Boston at a conference when she finally tracked him down. She outlined the situation as efficiently as possible and he confirmed her feeling that Rob and Rayna were in real danger.

"Look, Claire, the sooner you get this youngster out of there, the better. If you can get her to the US, I'll take it from there. I'll have to pull some strings to arrange the paperwork, but it can be done. I'm glad you called me. I can explain more later, but I've got to get back to the conference."

Much relieved, Claire thanked him and began to put together a plan in case she was able to persuade Rob to work with her, that taking Rayna to the US would be the right thing to do.

Rob had fallen into a deep sleep sitting upright on the couch, wrapped in the throw blanket. He was startled awake by the buzzing of his cell phone. Bleary-eyed he reached for the phone too quickly, awakening the pain in his ribs. "*Ja?*" he spoke gruffly.

"Rob? It is Claire."

"Hello," he said, trying for a more neutral tone of voice.

"I want to apologize for my behavior. I am not usually that, uh, rude."

"Think nothing of it. Are you back in the city?"

"Almost. I am on a flight stopping in France first. I will be in later this afternoon. Are you okay? You do not sound well."

Rob cleared his throat and sat up straighter. He tried to pull himself together, but he hurt all over and despite his best efforts a low groan escaped involuntarily. The anger and familiar frustration came flooding back. "I'm fine. Just... just a late night."

"How is the girl?"

"She's gone."

"Gone?"

Rob didn't elaborate, but merely replied, "Yes."

Suspecting he had not found an appropriate shelter for her, Claire persevered, "Do you want my advice?"

"No." Actually, he did, but not now. He was overwhelmed by pain and guilt and just couldn't deal with needing help. Not yet.

Recognizing that Rob was just being his own taciturn self, Claire didn't take offense and replied, "Fine, but we will talk further when I return. You are very stubborn."

That elicited a weak smile, "Yeah? So are you." He was grateful she seemed willing to let things slide for the moment.

"I am not stubborn, I am persistent. I will phone you again when I am in your area. You promised me a coffee."

"I promised you a coffee?"

Laughingly, Claire responded, "Yes, you did. I will talk to you soon. *Au revoir*!"

Although she had kept the tone of their conversation light, Claire knew that serious trouble for Rob was on the horizon. She knew him well enough now to suspect that he might act precipitously. He wouldn't involve the police. He would take action on his own and most likely would not plan things out or even let anyone know what he was about to do.

After her flight landed and she had finished her shift, Claire called Samir. He was closer to Rob than anyone else, and seemed to know him well. She could discuss the possibilities for Rayna with him, and maybe Rob would listen to advice from his buddy. In the meantime, she hoped that Rob had found someplace appropriate to take in Rayna.

Samir seemed to be more interested in socializing and matchmaking than social concerns, but Claire knew he was genuinely fond of Rob. He knew how impulsive Rob could be. Samir agreed that serious trouble was brewing, especially since he thought the swarthy man in Jan's office was indeed looking for Rob. Samir assured Claire that he would help in any way he could, just ask.

Claire's next call was to Daniel. She filled him in on the latest developments, including that the girl was no longer staying with Rob., but that she hadn't pressed him for further details. Although she was her usual calm, collected self, the concern was evident by her tone. Daniel's response did nothing to allay her fears.

"Wherever the girl is, she's not safe. Does this guy have any idea who he is dealing with? The traffickers won't stop looking for her and won't hesitate to use violence to get her back. I'm concerned for your safety as well, Claire. I wish you would back off from this, but I know you won't. That runs in your family, right? Advise your boyfriend to get himself and the girl out of there as soon as possible, and I'll help them both out, I promise. Keep me posted, Claire, and maintain a low profile."

She didn't correct him about Rob being her boyfriend, and she was secretly pleased to be compared to her mother and grandmother, who had lived such full, rich and meaningful lives.

It was a risk, but Claire decided to set the wheels in motion and got herself scheduled on the Amsterdam to New York runs. If Rob was ready for her help, she could arrange for him to be on a flight to connect with Daniel. If he didn't, well she would figure out something else when the time came.

After Claire's phone call, Rob just sat on his couch for what seemed to be an eternity, holding the phone in his lap. He looked around the sparse room and realized he hadn't heard anything from work. That was a good thing, right? He had slept dreamlessly through the night, and now a weak sun was already fairly high in the sky.

He had so many aches and pains, he couldn't count them. What should he do? A nice hot shower sounded like a good idea. But then he saw a knickknack lying on the floor where it had fallen under the table. He reached to pick it up, grunting and groaning a bit, but got it. He opened an almost full drawer to put it away.

On the top of the pile in the drawer, his glance was drawn to a photo in a now glass-less frame. It was the picture of his two pre-teen children. He stared at it for a moment or two, then took it from the drawer, ran his finger gently over the image and placed it out on the table. Memories of happier times with his precious children flooded through him. What kind of father had he been for them? How could he have let so much time elapse without seeing them?

As he began to close the drawer, he spied the old copy of the newspaper with the story of the dead girl. Something in particular caught his eye. An idea began to take form in his mind. He retrieved the paper from the drawer and studied the black and white, grainy photo closely. A group of looky-loos from the neighborhood was clustered behind emergency services and the open canal. In the background, he was sure he could discern a heavy-set lady who seemed familiar. He couldn't make her out too well, but his gut was telling him it was the fat lady from the airport. If he was going to trust his instinct he would need to take some action on his own, and damn the consequences.

Rob studied the photo for several minutes and re-read the article that described where and how the child's body was discovered. He figured it must be close to the place where she had been taken after the airport, if that was indeed the same fat lady. Could he find that place and the lady? And if he did, would he find Rayna there too? He wouldn't risk her life by going to the authorities, but he didn't think twice about risking his own by going out to find the lion's den and Rayna.

With a sudden burst of energy, Rob changed quickly, grabbed his winter coat, checked his pockets for his wallet and keys, took the old newspaper and rushed out of the apartment. When he tried to shut the door, it didn't close properly. He fiddled with the broken lock for a moment, and then went back into the apartment.

He retrieved his stash of emergency cash, stuffed it into his pocket. He removed the picture of his kids from the frame and carefully pocketed it. He swept his glance around the apartment. Did he have everything? No.

He went back to his bedroom, found his passport and stuffed that, too, into his jacket pocket. He closed the front door as best he could, turned and walked with determination out of the building where he had lived for the last three years.

# Chapter Eleven

Every detail of the photograph of where Naima's body had been found floating in the canal was imprinted in Rob's mind. He wasn't that familiar with the neighborhood mentioned in the article, but the photo revealed that the formerly regal residential row houses lining the canal were now rundown, and there was a small bar or pub on the corner. He was pretty sure he could find it, and figured it must be fairly close to the place that bogus "sister" and her nasty companion had taken Naima - and that was almost undoubtedly where he would find Rayna.

In his years of traveling as a salesman, whenever he needed to find out what was happening in an area, he'd find a local pub. Bartenders knew their neighborhoods and were a good source of information about what went on there. So that's where he headed when he left his apartment on that not-quite-sunny winter morning.

As he rode a tram and then walked several blocks further to the neighborhood, his memory bombarded him with images of Naima. She was so small, so obviously scared and yet strangely determined and, yes, even brave. Then pictures of Rayna floated through his mind. The dinner she had cooked for him; the way she had rearranged his apartment; her flirtatious ways. Finally, the image of her screaming as that thug dragged her out of the bedroom.

She hadn't been yelling for him like a victim, she just didn't want him to have walked into that terrible situation, or so he surmised. She hadn't wanted him to get hurt. How long had she been struggling against the two thugs before he arrived? From the aftermath that he had stepped into, he imagined she had put up a good fight. She was a tiny little thing, battling almost impossible odds.

He didn't attempt to devise a real plan. It simply wasn't his style. He just focused on how he would elicit the information he needed to find Rayna. That was the first step. Once he found her he would figure out what the next step should be. He did know his goal - to get Rayna to a safe place where she could be a kid or at least find the safety and nurturing that all children should have. Rob didn't think at all about his own safety. It was more important that he was finally going to start making things right, somehow.

He took care to make sure there wasn't an obvious sign of any shady-looking characters keeping watch when he arrived at the end of the block pictured in the newspaper photo. It was only eleven o'clock when he got to the corner pub so he was fairly confident there would be few customers.

As he entered the pub, he saw that his hunch was correct. There were only a handful of sketchy-looking customers, all men, and all seated separately at the small cafe tables that dotted a fair-sized, dark wood-paneled room. Rob's entrance was universally ignored. Along one side of the pub ran an actual bar, with shelves of various liquors on display behind it. A lone bartender, a young man who looked rather bored, polished glasses with a rag. Various black and white framed photos hung on the brown, stained walls and appeared to portray the history of the neighborhood and the previous pub owners.

Rob sauntered to the far end of the pub and grimaced as he took a seat in a creaky wooden chair at a table furthest from the door. The bartender, looking only slightly less nonchalant now, brought over a bar menu.

"Welcome to Cafe Brons. What can I get for you?"

"Uh, I would like to ask you a question."

"Of course."

Rob slid the newspaper over towards the bartender and tapped on the artist's sketch of Naima. "I'm following up on the death of this girl."

The bartender leaned over, studied the image and the headline. "Mm. I thought someone would be here sooner to ask about this."

"Oh?"

"Are you with the police?" Neither the bartender's face nor his voice gave any indication whether that would be a good thing or not.

Rob took a guess and hoped he'd picked the right answer. "No, I'm a--just a journalist."

"Well, then, you don't mind if I say what a lousy job the police did on this one?"

Rob sighed inwardly, relieved. "Not at all. Do you have a minute? I'd really like to hear what you know about this."

The bartender glanced around. Though no one seemed to need his attention, he hesitated. "Well..."

Getting the unspoken message, Rob placed a few Euro bills on the table and was rewarded with something that was almost a smile.

"I can spare a few minutes."

"May I borrow your pen?" The bartender passed over his pen and Rob continued, hoping he sounded like a reporter. "Thanks. As I understand it, the girl's body was found not far from here?"

"Yes, that's right, a bit away in the direction of the current, but there's been some ice so it wasn't far. I'm sure she was connected to the sex club down the street."

Inwardly Rob screamed in his mind 'eureka' while outwardly he managed to keep his voice sounding calm and dispassionate. "Why do you say that?"

"Simple. I leave work late at night, four days a week for the past couple of years. I've seen a lot of girls going in and out of number 527, all foreign-looking, not local kids. A lot of older men, too. Real busy place. It's not a daycare – not at that hour. And I know the neighborhood; it's my job to listen to all the gossip."

"What about a girl, about this tall--" He held up his hand to indicate Rayna's height. "Dark-haired, light eyes. Have you seen her?"

"I'm not sure. Like I said, there are a lot of girls going in and out."

"Do the police know about this place?"

The bartender laughed, but not in an amused way. "Of course. I've seen one or two of them visiting, too, even a few higher-up sorts, if you know what I mean."

Rob wasn't sure how accurate the information was, but he made some notes in the margin of the newspaper, as he imagined a reporter might. "How about an older lady, overweight, maybe British? Have you seen someone like that over there?"

With a knowing look, the bartender replied, "Yeah... two of them. Short, fat."

"Two?"

"They look like sisters. I don't know where they might be from. I can't hear them from here."

"And this girl, the one in the paper... an accident?"

"The press, no offense--"

"None taken."

"The press doesn't want to scare off tourists. Whoever is running that club has some powerful clients. Even if it wasn't an accident, I doubt you could ever prove differently, and in my opinion, no one cares."

As Rob nodded in agreement, the bartender noticed a customer beckoning him. "Excuse me," he said and went off to tend to his customer. Rob fidgeted while he waited for the bartender to return. Another patron entered the pub and sat at one of the tables, but didn't seem to take notice of Rob, much to his relief. The bartender brought the new patron a menu and hurried back to Rob's table.

"I'm sorry, I don't really have the time to chat more right now."

Placing a couple more Euro bills on the table, Rob replied, "Just one more thing..."

"Yeah, sure."

"I want to get inside. There is--the newspaper I work for wants photos. Do you know how I can do that?"

There was a slight hesitation and a shift in the bartender's voice, "What paper do you work for?"

Rob squirmed inwardly. "Oh, I still have your pen. Thank you." Rob quickly made what he hoped would be a distraction of returning the pen.

"Quite welcome." The bartender pocketed the pen, but stood still, waiting for the answer to his question.

There was no getting out of it. "Ah, it's a Dutch-American newspaper out of--in the mid-west U.S." Inside his mind he was panicking, trying to think of an answer that sounded plausible.

"Are you from there?"

"No, never been."

"Really?" The bartender's eyes became slightly squinted, as if this was starting to sound a bit far-fetched.

"Everything can be done over the Internet - but of course they want original photos to go with stories from...the motherland. So I was tasked with doing some undercover reporting, since I'm local." Rob silently took a deep breath to calm his nerves.

Another customer beckoned to get the bartender's attention. "Nice. Yeah, okay. You'll let me know when the story comes out?"

"Of course."

"Okay. Hold on." The bartender motioned that he'd be over shortly to the customer, searched quickly behind the bar, then returned and handed a business card to Rob. "Use this. It'll get you in the door, like a referral; just give it to the madam. But don't mention where you got it. And contact me at the bar when I can see a copy of the story. My name's Jeroen, but keep that between us."

"I always protect my sources, Jeroen. I'll contact you soon."

Rob reached out and shook Jeroen's hand, who now seemed quite pleased as he furtively scooped up the Euros on the table and pocketed them. "Good luck!"

"Thanks."

The pain in his ribs was still there, but Rob covered it as best he could as he got up and walked towards the exit. He was down a few Euros, but he felt quite satisfied with himself. He'd gotten the information he needed and even a sort of pass to get into the sex club.

Not bad, he thought, even if he had had to ask to borrow a pen. Some journalist! Oh well...

He checked his watch. It was still only lunch time. Too early to approach the sex club, he surmised. In the meantime, lurking around the neighborhood was probably not a good idea. Bertha or one of the thugs who knew what he looked like might be about and spot him before he made it inside. So he walked briskly out of the area, along the canal. As he recalled, there was a good place to get Middle Eastern vegetarian food not too far away. He'd duck in there, get some lunch and see if he could reach Samir.

By the time Rob reached the restaurant, he was really famished. He hadn't had any breakfast and at this point, he couldn't remember how long it had been since he had last eaten. He quickly found a table in a quiet corner, ordered falafel, and punched in Samir's number on his phone.

"Rob, where are you, man? Claire told me Rayna's gone. Did you find her a good place? You scheduled to work today?"

"I'm about to have a nice lunch in one of my favorite restaurants. Yes, Rayna's gone, kidnapped by a couple of thugs last night--"

There was a sound like a squeal as Samir interrupted, "What?!"

Rob tried to gloss that over, continued on in what he hoped was a calm, natural-sounding voice. "I'm not scheduled to work today. I'm looking for Rayna, and I'm pretty sure I know where to find her."

"Oh man! Please don't do anything foolish. These guys are dangerous. Nothing to mess with. You might have already have lost your job here. Don't risk your life. Contact the police. Let them handle this."

"Sam, I know you mean well, but you know as well as I do that the police won't do anything." He didn't mention the threat to kill Rayna if he contacted them. "The word on the street is that they don't just turn a blind eye, they are customers also at the sex club. I couldn't live with myself if I didn't at least try to rescue Rayna."

"I get it, but this is crazy. Look, you're gonna do what you think is best, and even though you won't listen to reason, I'm still your friend. Claire and I worry about you. If you get the girl, what then? Do you have a plan?"

A million thoughts swirled around in Rob's mind at once; none of them seemed like more than a vague inkling of a plan. "We have to get out of here."

"Yeah, lucky for you, we thought it might come to this."

Rob was too hungry to really focus, but knew exactly to whom the 'we' referred. He was relieved that Samir seemed to get him, but bothered that he and Claire were apparently plotting behind his back, perhaps expecting him to fail.

Luckily the feeling of relief won out as his falafel arrived. He accepted that perhaps with Rayna, in this situation, he was in over his head. He really needed some help from his friends, and not because he was incapable or unmanly. "Sam, do you have a suggestion?"

Samir did his best to keep his surprise out of his voice. "Uh, yeah. If you can get the girl to the airport, we'll get you out. Claire's got a good contact, that is, if you want her help."

"Yeah, all right. I'll call her after lunch. I'm going to try to get Rayna. I don't know how or when, but I'm going to give it my best shot. I'll get her, and we'll come there. I'll let you know whenever that might be. Thanks, Sam."

That handled, Rob turned his attention to enjoying a satisfying lunch that he hoped would provide the energy he needed to rescue Rayna.

# Chapter Twelve

As he walked the few blocks back to his destination – or was it his destiny? – light was fading from the sky and the soft shades of a winter evening settled in around him. There was still snow left in drifts along the edge of the sidewalk and against the buildings.

Rob kept his focus on the present moment. He refused even to contemplate making a plan. He would simply take one step at a time. He took the card Jeroen had given him out of his pocket, read the address again, and confirmed it corresponded to the next block.

He waited for a car emerging from that block to pass, then continued walking. Like many streets in Amsterdam, there were bicycles and scooters chained up or tethered to anything possible. There was just enough space to park tiny European cars in a tight row, and then an open drop into a narrow, murky canal. This part of the block was all residential, but most of the windows were dark and covered, revealing no signs of life. Rob saw no one else before he arrived at the house.

The house number was barely visible in the gloom, hand-written on a piece of paper taped inside a transom window. Yes, this was indeed number 527. It was an old building that had clearly seen better times. Despite its run-down condition, you could still see the architectural detail that had once distinguished it as a gracious home; the tall, narrow windows and a heavy, decoratively carved wooden door set into a brown brick facade. On the left, a tiny, dark alley cut through the row of houses, slicing the block in two. A small stone stoop, worn by the passage of time, led to the front door.

Even though it was early, the sunset was around 16:30 this time of year. A thick cloud cover had hastened the dusk and encouraged the temperature to drop even further. Rob took a deep, icy breath, steeled himself, and prayed that there was no one inside who would recognize him. He walked up to the door and rang the bell.

He waited a moment or two, panic and adrenaline coursing through him. He should have gone to the police. But they wouldn't do anything in time, not before Rayna might be killed or moved on somewhere else. If the police were customers, going to them and making a fuss would make it even worse. He could do this, must do this, himself. He had a goal, and somehow, some way, he would get Rayna away from this. That was his new mantra.

He almost jumped out of his skin when he heard a lock turn and the door was answered by a heavy-set woman. Rob froze, but it wasn't Bertha. This woman's appearance bordered on slovenly - a long skirt, stained blouse and short boots. She had a dust rag or piece of fabric in one hand, and was a bit out of breath, as though he had caught her in the middle of something.

An image of the woman who had met Naima flashed behind Rob's eyes. This lady looked to be a few years older and was wearing far less makeup, but there was definitely a family resemblance.

Not knowing how to greet her, Rob simply handed her the card Jeroen had given him. The fat lady glanced at the card, but said nothing. Instead, she stood aside and beckoned him into the house. She shut the door quickly behind him and he felt trapped, almost claustrophobic, although there was plenty of room.

The fat lady, the madam he presumed, ushered him through a dimly-lit hallway to a reception room that had once been an elegant drawing room. Now heavy red velvet drapes covered the walls, blocking out where there once might have been windows. Tacky accent mirrors gave the room a sexual fun-house feel. The wall to wall carpet was dark in color, almost like dried blood, and only served to make the room seem smaller than it actually was. An overstuffed plush red velvet sofa and love-seat were arranged near a massive sideboard.

The madam gestured for Rob to take a seat and finally spoke with a definite British accent, "Kin I getcha something to drink, love?"

His legs felt shaky, so he sat down quickly. "Uh, no. Thanks."

"Well, then, ya a wee bit early. We 'ave only a few on at the present. Are ya looking for somethin' special?"

Deeply uncomfortable, Rob could not bring himself to look directly at the madam. He shifted a bit on the sofa which was too soft, too cushiony and offered no support for his aching back and ribs. Eyes downcast, he replied, "Yes." It came out a bit higher in tone than his normal voice, so he silently prayed for his nerves to be steady.

The madam waited somewhat impatiently for a moment, then said, "Go on, don't be shy, love..."

"I, uh, prefer someone younger."

Winking, she replied, "I getcha. How much time wouldja like?"

"A half hour?" His voice came out sounding unsure. The room wasn't warm, but sweat was forming on his brow.

"I've got a few lovelies ya might fancy. If you 'ave time to wait, I kin have a selection 'round in fifteen minutes. How's at, love?"

"Yes, okay."

"By the way, love, it's a wee bit extra."

"Sure. How much?"

"Two hundred. Cash."

Rob got out his wallet, counted out crisp Euro bills, and handed them over. Without putting down her dust rag, the woman recounted the bills herself and then stuffed them into a pocket of her skirt.

"Yer money back if ya don't like what you see. If ya change yer mind about the drink, there's some refreshments over there." She gestured toward the massive mahogany sideboard that contained an arrangement of instant coffee, tea, sodas, and nuts. "I'll send the girls in as soon as they get 'ere. Just make yerself at home, love."

As soon as the madam left the room, Rob let out his breath, only now aware that he had been holding it. He started to sink back into the plush cushions, then groaned softly as the movement prompted the pain to flare up in his injured ribs. What the hell was he going to do for the next fifteen minutes? And if Rayna wasn't there? He silenced that thought.

He stood up, took off his jacket and laid it down on the sofa. He wandered over to the sideboard, perused the possibilities, but his churning stomach informed him it would be wise not to take anything. He fought down the nausea and returned to the sofa. He sat down on the edge, careful not to aggravate his injury. He tried a quick, silent meditation.

When the madam finally popped her head back in the door, it startled him and he jumped slightly. "Ready, love? In a minute I'll send in four; one at a time. Then I'll be back to see which one ya fancy."

Rob nodded and tried to swallow the bile that came up in his throat. The madam left him alone for a couple of endless minutes, with the door shut. He could hear only muffled sounds coming from the rest of the house, but couldn't identify them. He fidgeted, and noticed there were a few magazines on an end table. He selected one at random and leafed through it, not able to focus enough to read a single word.

His heart seemed to stop beating when there was a knock on the door. It was opened by a very young, petite Asian girl, perhaps around the same age as Rayna. She was dressed in a sort of school uniform - a white shirt with a dark tie, a short pleated skirt, long white knee socks, and Mary Janes. She had the mannerisms of a demure schoolgirl, with a soft giggle and one hand covering her red lips, but strode into the room, stopped in front of Rob confidently and struck a practiced pose, eyes downcast, as if shy. The magazine slipped from Rob's hand. He caught it, returned it to the table, and stood up in a rush.

"Hi." said the little girl in a soft, provocative voice.

"Hello."

"I'm Kazuki." She giggled again and put her fingertips over her painted lips.

To Rob, she seemed rehearsed and mechanical, which only heightened his sense of unease and alarm. "Uh... Nice to meet you, Kaz--?"

"Kazuki, number one, okay?" She held out an upraised finger.

Now he could hear her accent, but he wasn't sure if that was also part of the performance. Kazuki gave him a practiced smile and a bow. By reflex, he bobbed his head back at her. She winked and skipped back to the door, opened it and left.

Before Rob could react or sit back down or even breathe, there was another knock on the door and another girl walked in. It was Rayna. Rob's blood turned to ice.

She had taken a few steps into the room before she realized her next potential customer was someone she knew. She hesitated for a split second. Her eyes widened slightly, then her glance flicked up to a corner of the ceiling behind Rob. Somehow he understood in a millisecond.

He moved toward her and turned just enough so that he could follow her gaze peripherally. He caught sight of a partially concealed camera monitoring their interaction. His back was to the camera, but Rayna was in full view.

He silently willed her to play along, and coughed slightly under his breath to get her attention. "Hello, what's your name?"

Rayna started to speak, stopped, and shot another glance again at the camera. Rob positioned his body so that hopefully only Rayna could see his face, and not the camera behind him. He could only pray there wasn't another camera in the room as he raised his eyebrows to her.

Rayna understood and recovered her composure. She gave him her standard come-hither look, then announced, "I'm Rayna. Number two."

She still wore the denim miniskirt, but her short flat boots had been replaced by higher, heeled boots and she was wearing a sheer blouse over some kind of lingerie top. He could see a few bruises on her arms, evidence of the scuffle with the thugs.

"Rayna." It came out involuntarily, almost like a sigh.

As surreptitiously as she could, she glared at him. Yes, Rayna. Number two."

"Okay."

She flashed him her practiced, provocative smile, turned and sashayed out the door.

Within seconds there was another knock and the third girl entered. She had large dark eyes, olive skin, pigtails, and full red lips. She could have also been around Rayna's age, but looked older, as she was more developed. Her long lanky legs were barely covered by a short skirt, and she also presented as a schoolgirl or a Lolita in a partially unbuttoned white cotton shirt and starter bra.

"Hi, I'm Olivia." Her accent was also like Rayna's, Spanish in origin he thought, but from where exactly, he couldn't place it.

"Hello, Olivia."

"Number three."

"Okay."

She looked the part, but only managed a bored glance at Rob before she turned and sauntered to the door. She opened it, walked out, but held it open so the last girl could enter, then shut it behind her.

Rob was stunned, aghast at the tiny poppet who uncertainly entered. She was definitely the youngest of the girls, and looked like a living blonde-haired, blue-eyed doll, a pint-sized pageant princess in an ornate frilly dress. She had an adult hairstyle, complete with teasing and hairspray, but with soft tendrils left to cascade around her face. Full makeup with false eyelashes made her look perfect, save for her eyes. They were glassy and unfocused, and she seemed a bit unsteady on her feet.

Her voice was soft and sweet, but her pronunciation was mumbled. "Hawow."

Rob instinctively leaned forward, and his voice came out in an involuntary whisper. "Oh my God."

The girl looked around as though she wasn't quite sure where she was. She never glanced higher than the level of Rob's knees. She didn't seem nervous, just unfocused. She took a breath and tried again. "Hewow. My name is Angel, I'm nummer four." She smiled a perfect, practiced smile at Rob's knees, revealing capped, pearly white teeth. She curtsied with a slight wobble, and turned to leave.

An unseen hand opened the door for her, since Angel was barely big enough to do it herself.

Rob's hands involuntarily curled into fists, white-knuckled, as the bile rose again in his throat. His disgust and horror were almost overwhelming. He took a deep breath to steady himself. He could not succumb to his seething emotions. He needed to re-focus on the task at hand. He wanted to scoop that little girl up in his arms and take her to safety. But he knew that was just not a possibility, at least not now. He willed himself calm, uncurled his fists and pasted what he hoped would be an impassive look on his face.

He was about to sit down on the sofa when the madam entered the room. "So, love, which one strikes yer fancy?"

Rob straightened up and cleared his throat. "Uh... Number two."

"Okay, love. Lemme show ya to the room. Come along, now."

Rob grabbed his coat and followed the madam out of the room and down a long, narrow hallway. He was not a violent person at heart, but dark fantasies of slipping his hands around the madam's neck and choking her to death were irrationally present. He knew that wouldn't undo this atrocity, and there were certainly other people in the house who would be on the lookout for any trouble.

But in those few moments, as he followed the devil down the hallway, all his past didn't seem so important and he made a promise to himself for the future. He vowed to come back, to fix all of this, to save all the children he possibly could, though he had no idea how. At the moment, he still had yet to accomplish the rescue of one: Rayna.

The madam showed him into a small, dimly-lit room with the same red velvet, mirrored theme as the reception room. A large bed dominated the space. There were fresh towels and a digital clock on a side table along with a sex menu showing base prices and surcharges for extra time or services. Rob noticed a partly-open door that lead to a tiny en suite bathroom. He stood awkwardly, not quite knowing what to do.

"'Ere ya go. Relax, get comfortable, and I'll send in yer young lady in a minute." The madam checked her watch and compared it to the time on the digital clock.

Still in shock, Rob perched stiffly on the edge of the bed and laid down his coat beside him. He was at a loss for words. Not so the Madam. She fussed around the room, inspecting to make certain everything was clean and ready. She prattled on, "We get new ones in every couplea weeks."

"What?"

"The young ones, they go from club to club. There's a special membership, then we kin have exactly what ya like brought in, and ya have access to our other affiliates worldwide."

"Other... How much?" The thought was appalling, but he kept his composure.

"Good for a year, only a thousand cash. VIP status, and you get a discount for each visit."

Rob didn't blink, didn't breathe, just tried to keep going. "Maybe next time."

"If ya need more time today, just let yer girl know. Anything extra, it's all there." She pointed at the menu on the night table.

Too disturbed to speak, Rob simply nodded. The madam winked at him and left.

# Chapter Thirteen

Betta, the madam, and her sister Bertha were as close as two sisters could be. They were only a year apart in age and, when dressed alike, were often mistaken for twins.

The girls had grown up in London, in an area known for its gangs and hard living. They were neglected by their parents and left to run wild. Somehow Betta and Bertha's situation had fallen through the cracks in the social services system. Thus there had been little attention paid to their living conditions or upbringing.

Even though the family had a council flat, stability and a safe home life had not been the norm. There were visitors at all hours of the day and night, strangers who were buying or using drugs, and the girls never had a sense of routine or rules. The children just had to stay out of the way of adults to avoid beatings or worse.

The sisters relied on each other to survive, and together they developed fake IDs and schemes to avoid being taken into care or declared delinquent from school, and they did their best to stay out of police notice.

While other children were attending primary school, Betta and Bertha were shoplifting food and other necessities, something they both became quite good at. When they were barely into their teens, both of their parents died within six months of each other. Their father was murdered by a rival in a drug deal gone wrong, and their mother committed suicide after an AIDS diagnosis.

Although they had never been close to their parents, the loss at such a young age only exacerbated their bad behavior. Still avoiding social services and now without their family's flat, the sisters shuffled from relative to friends' homes - a week here, a month there. Bertha, the younger and wilder of the two, always ended up in some confrontation or conflict with their host that ended their welcome and made them homeless again.

Surprisingly, it was the less outgoing Betta who discovered how they could earn a living and finally live on their own, independent of adults or a government handout.

Both sisters had been the victims of rape and sexual abuse in the past. Now Betta coerced her sister into prostitution. Sex was going to happen to them anyway, so why not get paid for it?

Bertha loved the feeling of power. Where before she had been a victim, now she could control who touched her, and what she got for it. The sisters got their own flat and worked their way up from the streets into a private establishment with more exclusive clientele. For their teen years, they appeared to have risen above their impoverished origins. For a while, they reveled in their new life, spending huge sums of money on clothes and beauty services. Their hair, makeup and nails were always done, and they used a private car service when they were escorting. Their lack of education and strong working-class accents held them back from earning top dollar, but it was a far cry from what they had endured as children.

Neither sister had the foresight to plan for the future. People who grew up as they did, often didn't believe they would have much of a future, as death came early to so many. They put no money aside, nor did they attempt to educate themselves or learn any other job skill. As they grew older, their partying lifestyle turned into drug and alcohol dependence. The flush of youth and formerly slim figures that had earned them their independence were gone, and their working arrangement with the private establishment was terminated as they became unreliable and argumentative.

Betta became even more reserved as she fell back into depression. Now it was Bertha's turn to figure out how they might live.

One of Bertha's old regulars had connections to Bulgaria. He was no longer interested in her sexually, but he remembered her fondly and agreed to help the sisters out by providing his contacts to them. With him, Bertha concocted a plan to start their own brothel. Not in London, as the market was saturated and the competition was too well-established. No, their new place would be somewhere else, and cater not just to 'regular' clients but those who had a predilection for young girls. Betta, the more motherly of the two, would run the brothel, while Bertha with her more outgoing personality would do all the outside work which included working with contacts to locate girls and acquire the right customers.

The sisters became known in the sex industry, not for being glamorous or flashy, for those days were long behind them, but for branching out into more specialized areas and for taking care of their girls. Neither sister looked or sounded like a stereotypical madam, but both had brought their unique insight and understanding into the business, which flourished. They had saved themselves and come up from the streets, now they offered the same opportunity to those under their care.

They networked with other brothels, eventually moving to Amsterdam. Connections and payoffs were made to the police and politicians, and at first glance, they seemed to be running a legal business. There were very few people outside of the business who knew that there were underage sex workers connected to the sisters.

Betta, in particular, wanted to have the children stay with her, and when they weren't working they all lived together just down the street in a rented home. Unlike Bertha, she had always wanted to have her own family.

With the combination of years of abuse and physical excesses, both sisters were infertile. Betta doted on the children, as a foster mother might. She knew what it was like to be abandoned and unwanted. She at least had her sister. Many of the kids she cared for had no one at all.

Bertha was more concerned with earning a living, but did try to be sympathetic to her sister's wishes. She did her best to find children who were already working, and trusted her foreign connections to bring her the ones who they could rescue from the streets. Once they were in the club system, they were housed and given regular meals and a routine approved by Betta.

For some of the children who came from a lifestyle where they literally slept on the street and were frequently beaten and abused by johns, this was heaven. Bathing and grooming were done every day, and they were provided with clean, neat costumes for work. Betta performed well in her role as 'mother' tried to take care of the young ones, just as she had her sister.

Betta made sure "her" kids slept enough so that they never had bags under their eyes, and did not allow customers to bruise or mark them up in any way. She was reprimanded by her sister when she displayed too much affection or attachment to the children, but couldn't, wouldn't back down.

Bertha had a different approach. At the first signs of unwillingness or nervousness, she would administer just enough 'medicine' to help the children perform. She would also reward with junk food, something Betta feared would dull the children's skin, or worse, make them fat. Ironic, considering that the 'medicine' and junk food came out of both sister's stash of pills and crap food that they themselves still regularly indulged in.

But the sisters agreed on one thing; the kids they saw had already been working on the streets and were alone in the world. They were doing something good when they rescued these children from third world countries and brought them into their protected system with higher-end clients in upscale markets. The children never went hungry and were kept in far better conditions than where they had been. The sisters knew from experience how hard life was and knew they at least had always had each other. Betta even made sure that while in her care, her kids could get an education if they wanted which might give them the possibility of a future once they aged out.

Things had gone smoothly at first, but unfortunately, the sisters had gotten into a huge disagreement with their Bulgarian partner after they felt things had been mishandled. The Bulgarian didn't seem to care at all about the welfare of the children, something that particularly irked Betta. He had recently lost one of their children and visibly damaged another. That was unacceptable, even to Bertha. But the Bulgarian had personally hired all the muscle who protected the sister's brothel. They were loyal to the man who paid them, and wouldn't listen to Betta's pleas to resolve issues concerning the children in another way, without violence.

Worse still, Bertha had always thought that Betta was a little too soft on the young ones, and with the added stress the sisters had been bickering with each other more than usual. Betta wanted to cut ties with the Bulgarian completely and start over, while Bertha couldn't see their business working without their foreign connections; better to stick with the devil you know.

Thus behind the scenes there was a lot of tension. The future of the partnership and the business in Amsterdam was uncertain. Betta wanted to disappear with the girls but wouldn't dream of doing so without her sister's support. Anyhow, the Bulgarian had his goons keeping an eye on them, suspicious that the sisters might want to renege on their partnership. For now, though, the sisters stayed put.

# Chapter Fourteen

Still waiting in the small, red velvet bedroom, Rob took a couple of deep breaths, trying once again to steady himself. Outwardly he felt he looked calm, on the inside he was anything but. He'd thought he was a fairly sophisticated, worldly guy, but this was beyond anything he had imagined existed. Well, certainly not here, in this country. These were not women making a choice; they were children!

With great effort, he put his outrage aside to figure out what to do next. He stood up, searched around the room for a possible exit to the outside; a door, maybe, or a window. There were none, other than the door he had come through. Once he got Rayna, he hardly wanted to try and backtrack through the large house and out the front door. There had been an alley, and these types of grand old homes always had a back garden. That seemed like a better choice for a sneaky exit.

He entered the tiny bathroom, not much bigger than a closet, really. It too was decorated in red velvet wall coverings. He searched carefully and discovered a fairly good-sized window hidden behind one of the heavy drapes. He stared at it, trying to ascertain whether he'd be able to fit through it and how far a drop it would be to the ground. The darkness outside didn't afford him much of a clue.

He jerked, startled by a knock on the bedroom door, the pain in his ribs flaring. He returned to the bedroom as Rayna entered and ran to him. "Rayna!" was all he managed to say before she squealed and leapt into his arms. He tried to brace himself, block her from his injured ribs, but was caught off balance. He fell back onto the bed with her landing on top and the wind knocked out of him.

Straddling him, Rayna pinned his shoulders down on the bed and leaned over to whisper softly in his ear. "What you doing here?"

"I've come to get you out of here and to someplace safe."

"There is no someplace safe."

"You need to come with me. Trust me, Rayna."

"I think you dead! Now you risk life for me? They kill you for sure! I can live here okay."

Rob took as deep a breath as he could manage. "There's not a lot of time. I need to get you out of here."

Kissing him on the lips, she murmured, "I love you!" Despite his efforts to deflect her, she peppered his face and neck with kisses.

"Rayna!"

She stopped and, a hair's breadth above his face, stared into his eyes. "If they catch you, they kill you."

"I know. I am going to get you out of the country to a safe place. I'll be with you."

"Stay here with me."

"You know that's not possible, Rayna." He tried to recall everything Sam had mentioned earlier on the phone, and tried to make his voice sound as soothing as possible. "There is a place where you can safely live with other children - people your age. It's in America."

"I want to stay with you."

"I will visit you, but I must also find a safe place. Do you understand?"

"No." She looked as though she was either going to cry or throw something at him.

Rob groaned softly. "I can't leave you here, and I can't stay with you; be with you like that. Like this." He tried to gesture to indicate their current position, but the pain was hindering him.

Rayna's expression remained resolute and she continued to straddle him. Mustering all his strength, Rob picked her up clumsily and set her down at the end of the bed. He sat up next to her and gently rubbed his aching torso while Rayna continued to pout.

"I can get you to a better place than here. I can't stay with you. It's a place where there are other kids... kids like you. They can help you there, I promise." He hoped he sounded more convincing than he felt, but

Rayna remained motionless where he had placed her, and only stared at the floor in silence. Feeling the urgency of the situation building, Rob stood up with a bit of difficulty and glanced at the clock. "There's not a lot of time."

Finally, she answered. "Okay." But she still looked pouty.

"Yes?"

Rayna didn't look at him. "Yeah, I guess."

Rob picked up his jacket, reached into a pocket and pulled out a slip of paper and his cell phone and handed them to Rayna. "If something happens, if we get separated, you call this number. Claire will help you. She is the one who set everything up for you."

Distinctly unhappy, Rayna nonetheless nodded and took the cell phone and slip of paper.

"What do you have with you? Do you have anything? A coat?"

Rayna shook her head. So Rob handed her his coat. She put it on, stuffed the cell phone and piece of paper back in the pocket and looked up at him with wide eyes.

"Are you ready?"

She glanced at the bedroom door, as if expecting someone to come barging in at any second. "Why you do this for me?"

"I... I think it's the right thing for you."

"You good man." Tears welled up in her eyes and her lip trembled.

"You just have to trust me, Rayna. It's going to be okay."

Both of them jumped when they heard a noise from somewhere in the house. They stared at the bedroom door and listened for a long moment. Everything was quiet again.

"There's a place where no one will hurt you, where you'll be safe."

"In America..."

"Yes."

"I scared for you."

"Yeah, me too. But I promise I will get you to a better place." He noted that she wasn't afraid for herself, but for him. He held out his hand. Rayna took it and he led her into the bathroom.

At Rob's direction, Rayna closed the door. He rummaged through the fabric covering the walls and found the window he had noticed earlier. Rayna held back the curtain as Rob struggled to open the ancient window. He soon realized he would need some sort of tool to loosen the layers of paint holding it fast. "Is there anything kept in the room, like a screwdriver? Or something like a chisel?"

Rayna thought a moment, "No. Yes. A big dildo."

Rob froze, horrified. "What?!"

Rayna giggled at the look on Rob's face. "You no have plan?"

"Of course I have a plan. I just didn't think it through."

Rob continued his struggle with the window and winced at the pain in his ribs. Realizing there was no time to waste, he ordered, "Get the, uh, dildo and one of those towels."

Rayna hurried into the bedroom and returned seconds later with a giant rubber dildo and a towel. She handed them to Rob, suppressing the giggle that rose up at the sight of the blush that crept over Rob's face. "Stand back!"

There was no room for her to stand back, so she didn't move. Rob placed the soft towel over the window and bashed the sides of the window frame as quietly as he could, using the dildo like a rubber mallet. He didn't want to make too much noise or break the glass, alerting anyone who might be lurking in the old house.

Within minutes, the window came loose enough for him to open it. He peeked out and was relieved to find there was no one in the back garden outside and that the area below the window was unobstructed. "Come on. Stay close, and... just stay close."

Somehow, despite the pain in his ribs, he managed to hoist himself up and then squirm awkwardly out the window. It wasn't a far drop to the ground. He reached back to help Rayna.

Even wearing Rob's oversized coat, she was much more agile than he. She propelled herself easily through the window and landed next to Rob. He took her hand to guide her through the overgrown, unkempt garden, spotted here and there with drifts of snow and refuse.

# Chapter Fifteen

The narrow, walled backyard in which Rob and Rayna found themselves had obviously seen better days. The garden beds that had perhaps once held careful arrangements of flowers and shrubs were now overrun with brown, frozen weeds. A decaying brick path cut through the overgrowth, littered with cigarette butts. There was a heavy wooden door that led back into the house with the remnants of a plastic lawn chair next to it. Even in the frozen night air, the smell of recently smoked cigarettes was still fresh.

Rob quickly scanned around. The house appeared dark as all the windows were covered with the exception of the one they had just come through, although only a sliver of light showed through the drapes. The garden walls were tall, but there was a shorter back gate that looked like it led into another alley. It was partially obscured by scrub, and clearly hadn't been opened in years, but it was their only viable option. He tugged on Rayna's hand and led her silently towards the gate as quickly as possible.

Naturally, once they reached it, it was clear that the gate was both solid and securely locked. Undaunted by the pain in his ribs, Rob hoisted Rayna up and over the gate and began to climb over himself. Rayna was both light and nimble, but now he couldn't see her. He hoped she had landed safely in the dark alley beyond. She knew instinctively not to make noise, and seemed to trust him completely.

He was much less agile. He was cold without his coat, and his injuries had been aggravated by climbing out the window. His pant leg snagged on something, and that slowed him even further.

He was only halfway over the gate when he heard a noise coming from the house. "Hey!"

Rob turned and froze. In the dim light, he was sure he recognized one of the thugs who had beaten him at his apartment. The guy yelled something back into the house, sounding the alarm. Rob hesitated only a second, then adrenaline kicked in. He redoubled his efforts and managed to clear the gate, half falling to the ground in the alley behind the garden. He righted himself instantly, pain be damned, grabbed Rayna's hand again and they took off down the alley, moving as fast as they could.

The snow was piled high along the walls of the alley leaving only a narrow, icy pathway in the middle. Rayna's heeled boots kept her slipping and sliding, but she never hesitated. Several times she would have fallen if Rob had not held her up. Still, she stumbled and struck her knee, opening a gash. She only whimpered softly and limped on as fast as she could.

When they reached the opposite end of the alley, Rob paused and carefully peered out into the street. He didn't see anyone, and checked back the way they had come. Apparently, the locked gate and brambly brush had also slowed their pursuers. He could hear at least two angry voices cursing in a foreign language as they tried to force open the gate. They had not yet succeeded, but Rob knew they would soon be in hot pursuit.

They had maybe sixty seconds to think of an escape. Obviously, they couldn't outrun them. He led

Rayna out from the alley onto a narrow sidewalk to survey the possibilities.

This block had also seen better days. The street was overshadowed by looming residential townhouses on both sides. A couple of wan streetlights only managed to illuminate various states of disrepair, an uneven sidewalk, and potholes in the street. There were bicycles haphazardly parked everywhere possible, and a tight row of tiny, run-down parked cars on both sides of the cramped street.

Close to them was a cluster of bicycles. Keeping hold of Rayna, Rob desperately checked a few, but all were chained securely.

Rayna pulled him towards an unchained motor scooter. Within seconds Rob pulled out a plug and hot-wired it, and with some effort, kick-started the bike into life.

The sudden noise in the gloomy, quiet neighborhood only added to his sense of urgency. He sprang on the scooter and gulped to Rayna, "Get on and hang on."

She leaped on behind him and grabbed him with a death grip. He yelped as pain shot through his sore ribs and pushed her hands higher, away from the injury.

Rob gunned the engine and took off. On the icy sidewalk, the scooter shot forward abruptly and went into an unnerving slide, but as they caromed into the street, Rob gained traction and control.

However, they had only traveled a few meters when a car came barreling around the corner and headed straight for them. Rob's instincts warned him that this was the bad guys, and that they had caught up.

Rob spied an alley on his left and took a sudden, sharp turn into it. Rayna nearly flew off, but didn't. A fresh wash of pain coursed through Rob's body and he was sure his ribs would never heal at this rate.

He could hear the car's brakes squeal behind him, but the vehicle was too wide to follow them into the alley. Then, as suddenly as the car stopped, it took off again.

Anticipating that they would circle around to the other end of the alley, Rob braked hard. He told Rayna to get off, and she complied instantly.

The alley was too narrow to turn the bike around easily. He struggled to pick up the scooter and get it headed back in the direction from which they had come, and somehow, full of adrenaline, he managed. He jumped on and Rayna leapt on wordlessly behind him.

Rob glanced over his shoulder and saw the car arriving at the far end of the alley. One of their pursuers leaned out the window, tried to peer down the dark alley while he simultaneously yelled something into a cell phone. Rob couldn't place the language, but the tone was clearly threatening.

Rob gunned the little scooter's engine and shot back down the alley. They burst onto the street, skidded into a tight turn and were forced to brake suddenly. They just missed a full-on impact into a parked car by not more than a couple millimeters.

Rattled, Rob paused briefly, tried to steady his breathing then took off again at top speed. He didn't use his brakes or blinkers as he darted around cars and through cross streets into a busier part of the city. Drivers glared and honked, but he paid no attention.

Just as he was beginning to think they had lost their pursuers, he heard the distinct sound of a powerful motorcycle as it approached from behind at high speed, weaving through traffic with ease. Once again his instincts told him this was the enemy.

Rob sped into another narrow, icy alley, and then roared out onto a bumpy cobble-stoned street, but he couldn't lose the motorcycle.

They played cat and mouse this way until Rob reached the main part of the city where the streets were wider and clear of snow and ice. Now he had a new challenge as there was more traffic: taxis, trams and trucks intermixing with bicyclists, scooters and pedestrians. It was necessary to slow down as they darted around tourists and deliveries as well as other reckless drivers barreling through the chaos.

Although the traffic had slowed down the motorcycle as well, Rob could still hear it behind him. Their pursuer had the advantage of a more powerful engine as well as a helmet.

Rob knew he could not outrun him, but maybe he could outsmart him. The smaller scooter wasn't fast, but it was lighter and was also more agile, able to make much tighter turns. He guided it down steps, over pedestrian bridges, and along streets so congested they had to slip between parked cars and the open canal, hugging tightly to the very edge of the road. They sped through tourist-filled parks dotted with carts selling everything from Holland souvenirs to baked goods, the delicious scents making his stomach growl.

Every chance he could he'd turn sharply and suddenly, ducking into bicycle tunnels, weaving around obstacles or through red lights, narrowly avoiding accidents. Rayna was glued to him like a backpack, her legs and arms wrapped around him. Her hair and his jacket billowed out behind them as they flew past a thousand obstacles.

It wasn't long before their wild ride attracted the attention of the authorities. Two police cars with sirens blaring joined the pursuit. Now Rob and his pursuer needed to focus on losing the police, who were chasing them both.

"Hold on tight!" Rob managed to yell. It wasn't necessary - Rayna clung to him as if they were one person; she moved simultaneously with him to keep the scooter balanced after each swerve. It took all Rob's extraordinary skill to manage a sharp turn at high speed, in between two trams and traffic coming in both directions. They flew over a footbridge, landed hard and veered into another alley. Thwarted by the motorbikes' agility and unable to follow into the alley, the police cars fell behind. The sound of sirens dimmed, but Rob could still hear the roar of the powerful motorcycle, never too far behind them; and further still, the sound of the police sirens paralleling their course on the main roads.

Using every trick he had ever heard of, Rob followed a circuitous route. He managed to get them out of the city and onto the back-country roads that led to the airport. Following with a bit more caution, the motorcycle couldn't catch up, but did manage to copy every trick, and follow down every side street.

They had made it onto a clear, straight road with farmland and the occasional farmhouse or outbuilding. They had lost the police chase. But without a maze to navigate through, it would not be long before Rob's pursuer would easily catch up. He cursed under his breath and glanced behind them where he saw the motorcycle's headlight rapidly closing the distance. Rayna followed his gaze, her eyes wide.

Desperate, he veered sharply off the road and into a dark field. Rayna nearly fell off, but kept her balance and her hold on Rob. It took all he had to keep the scooter upright, going at top speed through fields, some still with vegetation or left fallow; others plowed with huge clods of frozen earth strewn at random. They bounced over ditches and ruts. Rayna screamed as they flew over a small irrigation canal. Rob yelled and cursed as they landed heavily, the jolt of pain from his ribs almost making him black out.

They were barely ahead of their pursuer when Rob's headlight and engine startled a flock of sheep. They continued straight through the middle of the randomly scattering animals, praying they wouldn't hit one.

Thick with winter wool and slow, the sheep scampered haphazardly behind Rob and Rayna, bleating in panic. Seconds later they heard a shout and then the distinct sound of a motorcycle upending, the engine gunning as wheels spun out into air.

Rob didn't pause or look back, just kept the little scooter going at full speed, never slowing as they cut back out onto a road. He didn't hear the motorcycle behind them, but maybe had bought them only a minute or two before the pursuit resumed. There was no time to waste.

It seemed like an eternity before the lights of the airport appeared. Still pushing the little scooter to its top speed, Rob steered them along an access road and finally into a gray cement airport parking garage. He finally slowed, guided the scooter off to the side and parked. His body was trembling, full of adrenaline and he couldn't quite control the shakiness of his limbs.

He took a deep breath and reached back to help Rayna get off. The scooter was trashed. It was still making little pinging and hissing noises that reverberated in the concrete garage, but at least they couldn't be seen from the road.

He assessed Rayna, still enveloped in his jacket, who seemed equally shaky. Her eyes were wide and wet with unshed tears. They were both coated with bits of brown vegetation, grime and soil.

He brushed her off, tried to smooth her hair and straighten her clothing. He noticed the gash on her knee. She stood still while he searched through his jacket pockets and found a tissue, but winced when he gently tried to wipe away the blood.

"Ow! You hurting me!"

"Sorry."

Their voices echoed in the garage; both of them sounded oddly hollow. Rob cleaned her as best he could, then traded the tissue for his cell phone. Rayna picked dirt and leaves from his clothing as he punched in Samir's number.

"Sam? New plan. Okay, just listen!" He muttered a curse under his breath as Rayna gazed up at him reverently, as if he was some kind of hero. "No, listen - I need your help right now. Go and open the side door, the one where everyone smokes. Yes, now. Claire..? Good. Go!"

He put the phone in his jacket pocket and turned his attention to Rayna. "No worries now. Come on."

He held out his hand to her and she took it. He inhaled deeply, willed himself to at least appear calm and collected, and straightened up as best he could manage. Rayna mimicked him, took a deep breath in and rose as tall as she could. Together they walked in sync out of the garage.

Rob led Rayna around the outside of a terminal, hugging the side of the building and avoiding surveillance as best he could. The route seemed to take an interminable amount of time, but they finally arrived at the side door without incident.

Rob knocked softly. The door opened and Samir popped his head out. "You're absolutely crazy, man."

"Just let us in, and you never saw us."

"No way." Samir sounded momentarily serious, but he made no effort to stop them. He gave a warm smile and a wink to Rayna as they ducked past him into a service corridor. It was empty, save for a bucket filled with sand and cigarette butts.

Rob and Rayna started to hurry down the long hallway as Samir shut the door securely behind them. He stopped them with an urgent plea. "Wait!"

"What?"

"Do you have your badge?"

Rayna stood silently, but gazed up at Samir through her lashes while Rob searched his jacket pockets. He found his security badge and I D. "Yes."

Samir shrugged off his uniform jacket and tossed it to Rob. "Take this!"

"Are you sure?"

"No, I'm not. You're really... leaving?"

"I was never here."

Samir looked at Rob directly, eye to eye. Rob reached out a hand, Samir took it, and then swung Rob into a hug. Rob groaned and Samir relaxed his grip. "Good luck, man."

"Thanks, Sam."

Samir nodded and trotted off down the service corridor, not looking back.

Rob put on Samir's uniform jacket, then used his security badge and a passcode to open a side door. He peered through cautiously. No one in sight. He motioned to Rayna. "We're almost there."

He slipped through the door and Rayna followed him like a shadow. He gripped her hand tightly as they hustled down maintenance corridors and service passages. A few times they had to halt their progress to avoid being spotted, but they emerged unchallenged from the last dimly lit conduit close to the ladies' toilet in the construction area.

Rob breathed a sigh of relief, retrieved his cell phone and made a call. "Hi, I'm here... I'm sure. Gate E7. Five minutes? Three? We'll make it!"

He slipped the phone back in the jacket pocket and scrutinized Rayna. She still looked disheveled and was breathing hard from exertion. His jacket looked the worse for wear. "Give me the jacket."

She stripped it off immediately and handed it over. He rolled it up carefully, making sure nothing would come out of the pockets, and tucked it under his arm. He tried to straighten up her tangled hair, but there wasn't enough time.

He took off Samir's uniform jacket, then his outer shirt and handed it to Rayna. "Put this on."

Rayna put on the shirt and buttoned it up as Rob shrugged back into Sam's uniform jacket over his undershirt. Rayna now looked like she was wearing a sort of shirt-dress, he supposed. At least she appeared cleaner and her see-through blouse was covered.

He placed his hand on her shoulder as they strode briskly into the main hallway. "Claire is going to help us get on a plane. I want you to pretend you don't know her, okay?"

"Okay." Rayna was clever enough to not only understand without question, but she also made the effort to relax her expression into something nonchalant and attempted to breathe as normally as possible. No one gave them a second glance as they moved quickly towards the departure gate.

As they arrived at the gate, the first boarding call had just been announced. A crowd of unruly passengers jockeyed for position in a vague semblance of a line. Claire stood firmly at the gate check-in podium alongside a younger, but matching counterpart, Marie.

Claire pointed out a well-dressed passenger to her and asked, "Marie, could you give the brochure on the frequent traveler program to the gentleman in the blue coat? I will handle this." She straightened a sheaf of papers, prepared for the onslaught.

Happy to oblige and somewhat relieved, Marie bustled off. She didn't notice as Claire waved Rob and Rayna to the front of the line.

Rob started to hand something to Claire, but dropped his rolled up jacket. It hit the side of the check-in podium. Startled, Claire dropped a few papers which fluttered to the floor. They both crouched down at the same time to pick things up.

"I am so sorry," she said.

"No, it was my fault."

When they stood up, Claire had his winter jacket and he had her pile of papers. They made the exchange and Claire scanned the papers Rob gave her, as she would for any transport paperwork.

"It looks good. Here." She handed him back a few papers.

He raised an eyebrow, but no one behind them was the wiser. Claire smiled a well-practiced, professional grin at them both. "You can take her on board now. Have a nice flight, young lady."

Rayna remained silent and had managed to appear almost bored or uninterested. Again, no one gave them a second glance.

Rob and Rayna walked down the boarding ramp and onto the plane. Claire turned to the next passenger in line and checked his boarding pass.

When Marie returned to help, Claire murmured to her. "Are you okay on your own here, Marie?"

Marie merely nodded as the sea of passengers rolled toward her.

Claire hurried down the boarding ramp to catch up with Rob and Rayna. It seemed like hordes of passengers were swarming onto the plane, anxiously looking for their seats and trying to stuff their overpacked carry-on baggage into the cramped overhead bins.

Claire slipped expertly through the throng and had almost caught up with Rob and Rayna in the central galley, but Simone, a novice flight attendant, beat her to it. Addressing Rayna, Simone said, "Welcome aboard, young lady." Then she turned to Rob, "May I see her paperwork, please?"

Caught off guard, Rob stalled as he pretended to be searching for Rayna's passport and transfer paperwork. When Claire reached them she was slightly out of breath, but she managed to give the illusion of complete self-control and coolness. "I will take care of this one, Simone. We are missing the vegetarian meals." Claire held out her hand to Rob, who gave her back the papers she had given him earlier.

Simone's smiling expression cracked a bit, and she looked slightly confused. "No, everything came in two minutes ago."

"Oh? Good. Is the coffee machine in the back galley working?"

"As far as I know. Was there a problem?"

Claire pretended to scan Rob's paperwork and replied, "Someone mentioned that there was. Could you check to see if it has been fixed?"

"Certainly." Simone left the central galley and squeezed slowly through the throng of passengers toward the back of the plane.

Claire breathed a sigh of relief and glanced down at the sheaf of papers in her hand.

Rob asked, "What is that?"

"It is the paperwork requesting a shift change. Actually, it is not mine. It belongs to the new gate agent."

Chuckling, Rob replied, "You're very creative."

"Why, thank you, sir." Claire gave him a mock curtsy and a genuine smile.

Rayna glared at them. Claire snapped back to a more professional demeanor and turned to rifle through an employee cabinet. She fished out a baseball cap stored there and handed it to Rob. "Put this on after I seat you, and give me your uniform jacket."

Still smiling and oblivious to Rayna's umbrage, Rob nodded and then asked, "Which way?"

"Business class," replied Claire and led them toward the front of the plane and the first class cabin, where only a couple of passengers were settling themselves into the roomy seats. She stopped at two seats on the empty side of the cabin, and indicated for them to be seated.

As surreptitiously as he could, Rob took off Samir's uniform jacket and handed it to Claire. He kept his own jacket and slid into the window seat. Rayna sat next to him. As instructed, he put on the baseball cap and pulled it low over his eyes, transforming from uniformed employee to just another unremarkable passenger.

Claire rummaged through the overhead bin, pulled out a blanket and pillow and handed them to Rayna.

"Here you are, *chérie*. Get some rest. I will be back to check on you. Economy is full, but there are not many more coming up here."

Rob and Rayna buckled their seat belts. Rayna spread the blanket over herself, then grabbed Rob's arm and snuggled against him.

As she had thousands of times before, Claire recited a pleasant, "Enjoy your flight."

A first-class flight attendant entered the cabin carrying welcome champagne for the other passengers. He was much younger than Claire, and appeared to be as inexperienced and flustered as Simone. Claire raised her voice slightly and directed an efficient smile at him, "I already took care of these passengers over here, Raymond."

He nodded his thanks at Claire and hustled to serve the champagne while he took mental note of a flood of requests for items from the reading selection, headphones, and snacks.

Claire leaned over and whispered, "Just pretend you are asleep, and I will make sure Raymond stays busy helping other passengers." Rob's mind was transported instantly as he caught a whiff of Claire's lavender scent. He turned his head to watch as Claire retreated briskly down the aisle and out of the business class cabin.

His attention was regained when Rayna pulled his arm closer to her over the armrest. Only after takeoff did it feel like he could start to breathe regularly again. Rayna snuggled closer with her head on his shoulder and seemed to doze off almost instantly. Rob stared out the window at nothing in particular. The adrenaline rush that had kept him going for so long faded away. Every muscle and bone in his body ached. He could take no action at the moment to distract himself, and felt uneasily alone with his swirling thoughts.

He had not allowed the thought of failure to even cross his mind, but now that he and Rayna were safe, the real danger they had both escaped hit him hard. What had he been thinking? Samir was right. He had been crazy.

But they had made it. He didn't know what the future would hold for him, but at least he was sure Rayna would no longer be exploited as a sexual object. She would be cared for and helped to heal.

She deserved this chance for a new life. She had demonstrated courage and savvy during their wild escape. Never once did she complain and she had followed his instructions without a peep. She was a fighter, a real survivor. He was... proud of her.

With that thought, his eyes drifted closed. He wouldn't have to pretend to be asleep. He was.

Four hours later Rob stirred. He could not get comfortable. The aches throughout his body gradually woke him. For a second he wondered where he was, and then the drone of the plane's engines reminded him. Rayna still slept, snuggled securely against his shoulder.

Gently, so as not to wake her, he disentangled himself, got up, glanced around and saw that the few other passengers in the cabin were either sleeping or had headphones on. Either way, they paid him no mind.

He glimpsed Claire as she stood in a small forward galley. She flashed him a smile. Had she been watching him sleep? He found that thought to be oddly comforting. He double checked to make sure Rayna was still sleeping and then went to join Claire.

She pulled the door curtain over enough to give them a bit of privacy, but left just enough of an opening so she could observe anyone coming down the aisle. She poured a cup of coffee for herself and handed Rob a cup of tea, which he gladly accepted.

"She looks okay. I think she's actually sleeping, without nightmares."

Claire responded simply, "I admire what you have done."

"Thank you for... everything." Rob looked down at the floor, took a sip of tea. He didn't know how to properly express his gratitude, and the relief that he felt was overwhelming.

"What will you do now?"

"I... I hadn't really thought about it."

Claire laughed. Teasingly she pointed out, "At least you are consistent." She hadn't meant it in a mean-spirited way, but she noticed that Rob did not share her laugh. He still appeared to be embarrassed, so she quickly sobered. "I can see that you are willing to give up your life for that girl." She spoke from her heart, and the warmth in her voice touched Rob deeply.

Feeling somewhat undeserving, he blurted out, "No one else would do anything."

She knew that he meant the authorities, not her or Samir, so she didn't take offense. "The hero with half a plan."

That brought a crooked smile to Rob's face, but he continued in earnest. "I'm sorry for dragging you into this, again."

"It was my choice." Her words were strong and clear.

They stood together in silence for a moment. There was a little turbulence. Claire automatically steadied her coffee cup. Rob peeked through the curtain to check on Rayna, who appeared undisturbed.

Claire followed his gaze. "There are many more like her."

Rob turned back to her. "You've been talking with Sam?"

Claire replied with a smile. "He has been my friend, too, for a while."

Rob's response came out a little harsher than he intended. "I couldn't just mind my own business this time and let the situation continue."

"Do you regret your actions?" This was just a gentle curiosity. Claire knew his upset was not directed at her.

Rob shook his head. He gazed at Claire, and she could see the fire in his eyes, hear the conviction in his voice. "Not at all. I wish I could do more. I wish I could have helped the first girl. I can still remember her face and that look of fear in her eyes and then the exact same look in Rayna's eyes. Claire, she was just a child!" As memories of Naima flashed through his mind, he shivered slightly.

To give him a moment to recover his composure, Claire stirred her coffee and then asked if he would like sugar in his tea. He declined it, as expected, and she busied herself tidying up the spotless galley. "If you need a place to stay until you get... things together..."

Rob smiled, catching her drift. "You have an apartment you're not using."

"After this..." Claire waved her cup vaguely in a circle, "I may be taking early retirement."

Rob laughed, and then sobered quickly, "I'm so sorry."

"Yes, you mentioned that. A toast to the future, and Rayna's future!" Claire raised her cup and Rob joined her. Then Claire passed along a brochure of the shelter and treatment program. Rob glanced at it briefly. It almost looked like it could be for a summer camp, except it was staffed with child development specialists and trauma counselors, psychotherapists and holistic practitioners of various modalities. The center was located on a private nature reserve in the mid-west part of America, and it looked quite picturesque. He tucked the brochure away for later, not wanting to think about the future, or Rayna being gone.

Rob and Claire spent the next hour talking about everything but the situation at hand. Instead they shared happy childhood memories, their favorite foods and travel locations, and what books were on their 'must read' list. Through it all, Rayna slept peacefully, lulled by the gentle motion of the plane and the white noise of the engines.

# Chapter Sixteen

Claire checked her watch and was surprised by how quickly the time had flown by while they were lost in conversation. She retrieved two vanity bags from a cabinet and handed them to Rob. "There is one for each of you. Combs, toothbrushes, that sort of thing. I thought you would like to refresh yourselves before we land." She turned to a small medical kit and handed over an adhesive bandage and an antiseptic wipe. "This should help too." She turned to exit the galley.

"Claire..." Rob's voice caught. Claire waited for him to continue. "...Thank you." He couldn't say any more. It was the smallest things that now felt overwhelming. Claire just nodded and smiled. She held the curtain for Rob as he lumbered back to his seat next to Rayna, undone by a simple gift of sundries.

Claire left business class, and Rob sat down heavily in his seat, holding the bags. Rayna looked so peaceful; he was loath to wake her. So he just sat for a minute, lost in thought.

He was powerfully drawn to Claire, but not just because she was attractive and well put-together. She was smart and kind - clearly the type of woman who thought about others and how she could be helpful to them. She had put her career at considerable risk to help him and Rayna. She had also gently chided him for his impulsiveness and lack of planning - so different from her own disciplined attention to detail and strong networking skills. But she had never made him feel the fool.

A sudden realization washed over him. He had no place to live, no job, and no plan once he had handed Rayna off to the people who would get her into the country and take her to the shelter. Claire had suggested he could stay at her apartment in Paris, but he would need an income, a purpose. He had no interest in mooching off of someone else. What could he even offer a woman like Claire? She had her future planned out, and he couldn't see beyond tonight.

Rob didn't have any answers, so he turned his attention back to the moment. He gently nudged Rayna awake. She had slept almost the entire flight. Her eyes were bright and she smiled up at him in a way he had never seen before. As disheveled as she was, she gazed at him with such trust and certitude that his heart skipped a beat. His mind was filled with a similar image from a long time ago when his own daughter had looked at him in that way, when he could have taken care of all the scary things in the world and kept her safe.

He shook his head to clear his mind. This was different. He handed Rayna a bag of sundries. "Let me take a look at your knee." Rayna sat quietly while he cleaned her wound and applied the bandage. They went together to the lavatories and both emerged minutes later looking a sight better. They returned to their seats just as the captain announced their approach to the airport.

Rayna seemed suddenly nervous. She grabbed Rob's hand and held on tightly. "What you do with me now?"

Rob did his best to answer; he showed Rayna the brochure from the shelter and explained how Claire had arranged things for her. Rayna looked dubious, but didn't say anything more as the plane landed and rolled to a smooth stop.

They had no luggage to collect, but Rob tried to seem busy as most of the other passengers deplaned. Finally, Claire came to join them, and they exited the plane together.

Claire glanced around the airport gate area and, through a crowd of travelers, spotted the man she was seeking.

Daniel Garcia was quite the distinguished-looking gentleman. He was older, maybe in his sixties, but had clearly been tall, dark and handsome all of his adult life. Nowadays he kept his salt and pepper hair neatly trimmed, and sported a pair of dignified spectacles. He was wearing a conservative tailored suit and his broad shoulders exuded confidence. Rob suddenly felt short and bedraggled. A momentary tinge of jealousy flickered through him and he scowled without realizing it.

Daniel spied Claire, nodded, and discreetly signaled to two equally handsome, suited agents. They materialized out of the crowd and ushered Claire, Rob, and Rayna to a side room off the main concourse. Daniel followed close behind.

Noticing the look on Rob's face, but mistaking its meaning, Claire whispered, "It is okay, he is someone I trust."

The room they were escorted to was well-lit and simply furnished with a pair of couches, several comfortable-looking chairs, and a conference table. There was a kitchenette area with a small refrigerator and a coffee maker. A basket on the counter offered bags of chips and various other packaged snacks.

Once they were all seated, Daniel announced, "Welcome to America. I'm Daniel Garcia, this is Tony and that's James." He smiled at Claire, and his tone warmed noticeably, "Nice to see you again, Claire."

Claire's tone was equally warm as she answered, "Likewise. This is Rob, and of course, the young lady is Rayna."

Daniel got up, walked over to Rayna and crouched down in front of her to introduce himself at eye level.

Rob couldn't help himself. He leaned over to Claire and muttered, "How well do you know him?"

Her eyes sparkled with mirth as she got the reason for his frown. She whispered back, "Relax... we are just friends."

Daniel spoke to Rayna in a soothing, gentle tone, "We're going to help you get into the United States, and we have a wonderful place for you to stay, Rayna."

Rayna did not reply, but managed to look both terrified and defiant at the same time. Unfazed, Daniel asked, "Would you like a soda?" She gazed at him wide-eyed and nodded.

He got up, fetched a soda from the refrigerator, grabbed a bag of chips from the counter and handed them to Rayna. She still didn't speak, and turned her attention to opening the soda and chips, consuming them as if she hadn't eaten in ages.

Daniel returned to official mode and strode over to Rob, "You and Claire will not be allowed to go with her any further." He turned to Claire and his demeanor softened. "I apologize. I didn't make the arrangements myself."

"I understand." Claire smiled coyly up at him and by habit smoothed her uniform.

Rob interrupted. Asserting himself, he said, "I want to be kept informed as to how she's doing."

Snapping back to his professional nature, Daniel replied. "No problem. We can help you with future visits to the treatment center or you can arrange travel visas and so forth on your own."

"Thank you." Rob still felt a bit put off, and there was a moment of silence as he got lost in his thoughts.

Daniel's baritone suddenly boomed in the room and startled Rob's reverie. "Everything has been arranged for her ongoing care. If there's nothing else...?"

Looking over at Claire, Rob sputtered, "I, uh..."

She filled in adroitly, "He needs to get to Paris."

"Ah..." Daniel raised an eyebrow as he assessed Claire and Rob. Rob shifted in his chair and looked down at the floor, following only some of the subtext. Daniel chuckled as Claire smiled and winked at him.

"Well done, Claire. I can make that arrangement. Before we part ways though, I'd like to speak with you privately, Rob."

Rob looked up, surprised, and replied automatically, "Sure. Okay."

Daniel walked over to Tony and spoke softly, "Please get the ball rolling for Rob's trip to Paris." Then with a nod, he signaled James, who got up, walked over to Rayna and crouched down in front of her.

"Hello, Rayna. I'm James." Rayna continued to munch on her chips as she looked him up and down. "I'm going to be bringing you to a very nice place. Is that okay with you?"

Rayna looked over at Rob, almost as if she was asking for his permission, and she still didn't seem too happy. He had somewhat conflicting emotions himself, but tried to make his voice sound reassuring. "It's okay. You'll be safe and well-cared for." He glanced over at Daniel, who nodded his agreement. Rob continued, "I'll visit you as often as I can."

Rayna dropped the chips, leapt out of her chair and ran over to Rob. Anticipating her actions, Rob had stood up and braced himself. She hurled herself at him and threw her arms around his waist, hugging him fiercely. He grimaced then hugged her, patted her gently on the head, and smoothed her hair. "Trust me, Rayna. It's going to be okay."

They stood together for a wordless moment. Then Rayna looked up at Rob and nodded her assent, tears welling in her beautiful eyes.

James came over and touched Rayna gently on the shoulder. "Ready?"

Rayna reluctantly released her hold on Rob and took the hand James held out to her.

Nearly moved to tears herself, Claire rose, picked up the fallen chips and soda and followed Rayna and James to the door. Rayna turned back to gaze at Rob one last time. He straightened, fixed a smile on his face and waved to her.

When the door closed behind them and Rayna was gone, Rob sank heavily into a chair.

"Do you need a minute?" Daniel's deep voice brought Rob back to the moment.

"No, I'm okay." And just like that, his mood lightened. They were all safe, the ordeal was over.

"Claire has a brochure from the treatment center. It will be a wonderful, supportive environment for Rayna."

"She gave it to me on the plane." Rob sat up straighter in his chair and continued, "I feel pretty good about the whole thing, like I made a difference in a child's life. Now Rayna has a chance for a real future."

"I know that feeling. Would you like to do it again?"

Without hesitation, Rob looked directly at Daniel, "Yes."

"We need people like you who are willing to help at the ground level, rescuing children and helping to bring their traffickers to justice. As a 'consultant,' you would be an independent contractor, able to go places and do things that I, as an agent of the U.S. government, cannot. You would not be working for us, but with us. Understand?"

"I'm in!" He really didn't have anything much to lose. He had to assume he wouldn't be welcomed back to his job at the airport, nor would it be safe to return to his apartment or even Amsterdam. He instinctively knew the opportunity Daniel was offering would be good for him.

He didn't try to analyze why, and didn't ask any questions. As usual, he simply acted impulsively in the moment, blurting out his answer in a breathy rush.

Daniel took the lead and continued the conversation. "Look, the way you went about things was a bit... haphazard, but you demonstrated courage and commitment."

Rob's rush deflated a little and he couldn't quite look Daniel in the eyes. "I guess, but I couldn't have done all this without Claire's help, and my friend Sam. I definitely couldn't have done it alone."

"That's what I'm offering. You'd be working with other organizations. There would be a plan, certain protocol and laws to follow, but you'd have support. For now, you'll need to keep some distance from your old life and identity." Daniel removed a document from his suit pocket and slid it over to Rob. "These are a few contacts who can help you establish a new identity. I understand you'll be staying with Claire for a while."

Again, Rob felt a bit embarrassed. "I, uh, yes. Her apartment."

Daniel stared down Rob, waited while he glanced at the list of contacts and then refocused his attention. "Claire is one of the best people I know. I don't want you to ever put her in this type of situation again. Even if she offers, I want you to come to me, first. Clear?"

Ashamed, Rob's voice came out a bit higher than normal, and in sharp contrast to Daniel's self-assured baritone. "No, I won't. Yeah. Yes." He took a deep breath and willed himself to be calm and his voice steady. "Can you tell me something more about where you're taking Rayna?"

"It's one of several recovery and treatment centers for children located around the world that we can place our rescues in. It's located in a country setting, and similar to a summer camp. It provides a safe and structured live-in environment for kids ages 8 to 18. If the child progresses enough, they are then placed into a specially trained off-site foster family. Many of our rescues can be integrated into normal life and normal schools and go on to be successful, healthy adults. Quite a few of the therapists and doctors on staff are former rescues themselves."

A knock on the door interrupted. Tony came in bearing a sheaf of paperwork. "I've got everything necessary to get you back to Europe." The collection of documents was intercepted by Daniel who glanced over the legalities before passing them along to Rob.

"I owe you, well, everything."

"No. You saved Rayna's life, and in doing so gave up your own. I'm looking forward to our working together in the near future. You get settled first, and use the contacts I gave you. In the meantime, don't hesitate to call me any time with any questions. Take care and be safe."

Daniel stood up and Rob followed his lead automatically, expecting a handshake. But Daniel grabbed him in a man-hug, clapping him on the back robustly enough to restart the ache in his ribs. Although surprised, Rob held his composure until both Daniel and Tony had exited the room. He then sank back down into a chair and reflected on the sudden turn of events that had so changed the course of his life. Indeed he was being given a second chance at it, with more purpose and meaning. Still, in the shadows of his mind was the guilt he felt about Naima and all his other failures in life. Well, his old life. He couldn't go back, that was certain.

Rob stood up, resolutely squared his shoulders, and checked the paperwork for his departure gate. There was nothing else he could do but move forward. With that thought, he strode as confidently as he could out of the room and towards the future.

## *Two Years Later*

Rob sat on a nondescript bench in the Taiwan International Airport. There were multitudes of signs and advertisements in different languages. It could have been an airport in Brazil, or Bangladesh, or Thailand.

He'd been in all of them during the past two years since he began work as an independent consultant. While Daniel was constrained by jurisdiction lines and governmental cooperation, Rob could go and track down traffickers in their home countries, find them before they could put the children on tour and fly them around the world as sex commodities. He was good at his new job, and his natural ability to blend in and look inconspicuous had served him well.

Like many seasoned travelers, he was casually dressed and relaxed, his shirt tucked into his jeans, a leather jacket over his arm. He sat in the waiting area for a flight to Amsterdam that would soon be boarding. He would not be boarding of course. With all their local connections, Rayna and Naima's traffickers had disappeared underground shortly after he had gotten Rayna out of the Netherlands. He wasn't going to risk going back home until they were caught and brought to justice.

Now he lived in a small apartment in Mechelen, in the Dutch-speaking part of Belgium, close to the airport in Brussels. He had stayed at Claire's for only a short while until he was able to set up his own place. It really wasn't all that different from his old apartment in Amsterdam. He still liked it to contain only the basics; what was necessary. He traveled a lot for work, gave talks and presentations about child trafficking, and met with governments and NGOs to create solutions to make a difference.

He did keep a couple of framed photographs on display, though. One was of his children when they were young; the other was of him and Samir, smiling together after a night out.

As unlikely as it seemed since their personalities were so different, their friendship had continued. They would meet in Brussels and Samir would drag him off to a trendy club and catch him up on all the latest gossip. He felt grateful as he remembered how Samir had loaned him his uniform jacket the night he fled with Rayna. Claire had managed to return it to him with no one the wiser. He really owed them both everything. They were an unlikely trio; so different from one another, yet their friendship had remained strong.

Ah, Claire, he mused. Their common commitment to reducing child trafficking on international flights served to strengthen the bond between them. Not long after she had played such a critical role in rescuing him and Rayna, she had retired. She had become an ardent advocate for training flight attendants in how to spot potentially trafficked victims and how to handle the situation when they did. She was putting her considerable planning and organizing skills to use in forming a non-profit to provide that training.

And Rayna. She seemed to have adapted herself well to her new life. She was attending school and had been placed in a foster family. She had also started looking towards the future. Every time he spoke with her she wanted to study something different. First she had wanted to be a chef, then a professional singer or a makeup artist. Now she wanted to be an interior designer.

He smiled to himself thinking about her joy and passion for everything, even after what she had lived through.

Rob leafed through a magazine, his musings interrupted by a photo concealed within its pages. He had taken it with a telephoto lens after tracking down a notorious trafficker. She had been quite proficient at her trade back in the day, but her influence had been waning over the years. She could still afford to pay off the local police and politicians, but an economic downturn had made her start looking outside the country to the wealthier nations to ply her trade. Word on the street was that she didn't trust anyone else, and would accompany the children herself to their destination.

He studied the photo of the older Asian woman and casually scanned the crowd of travelers. When he spotted the older woman in the photo, he stood up smoothly, nodded to the side of the main hall and flicked his gaze back to the woman. She was carrying a large handbag in one hand; the other held the hand of a small girl.

Daniel, along with two uniformed Taiwanese police officers, a male and a female, suddenly appeared out of nowhere and moved swiftly to position themselves around the older woman and young girl. Without incident the officers quietly herded their target into an unused private waiting area, blocked from public scrutiny.

Rob joined them. He and Daniel took out the badges that identified them as part of the International Anti-Child-Trafficking Task Force as the male officer addressed the older woman in her own dialect, "Chen Mai, you are being arrested for child abduction and child trafficking. You are not obliged to say anything unless you wish to do so, but what you say may be put into writing and given in evidence."

Chen Mai responded by spitting at him as she struggled to free herself from his firm hold. Undeterred, he simply turned her around, cuffed her and led her away through a back door.

The female officer bent down and spoke reassuringly to the young girl in a dialect. The child looked at her wide-eyed for a minute, her black eyes peeking out through straight black hair and bangs. She was thin and petite; a tiny little thing with porcelain skin and a button nose. She replied hesitantly, and then took the hand the officer had extended to her.

Together they walked over to Daniel and Rob. The officer's perfect English was tinged with feeling. "She's an orphan from the Guangdong province. She's eight years old and her name is Lin. We can get her into the social service system, but her prospects here are not good. Orphanages here are overcrowded, and there's not enough money..."

Daniel spoke up immediately, "I will make arrangements to have her brought to a shelter with a treatment program in another country."

Rob interjected, "Does she speak any English?"

The officer leaned down and conferred with Lin. There was a short reply from the wide-eyed child. The officer straightened up. "Only a few words. I can stay with you until her travel clearance comes through."

Rob moved to stand next to the girl, "I saw an ice cream shop nearby - would you like an ice cream, Lin?"

When she heard the translation, a shy smile crept over Lin's face. She nodded her head. Rob reached out a hand; Lin took it. Along with the officer, they walked together out into the main concourse followed by Daniel. They paused at the side of the shopping area, just short of the ice cream concession.

Daniel smiled warmly at Rob. "Take your time. I'll give you a call when the clearance comes through and we're ready to proceed. Good work."

"Okay, thanks."

"The next case is in Germany. We are with Interpol on this one... unofficially of course."

"Of course."

Daniel clapped him fondly on the shoulder and strode off.

Rob removed his badge as he and Lin along with the officer blended into the crowd and made their way to the ice cream shop. The little girl's hand felt clammy, but she gripped him with conviction. She was so young, and clearly had been through a lot. Her fear was palpable, but so was her pluck and Rob knew in his heart that she would be okay.

He put those thoughts aside in the ice cream shop and instead quietly observed as Lin ogled the wide array of flavor choices and toppings. Her eyes grew even wider and her smile bigger at the sumptuous display before them.

He might have been reminded of a past memory, but he stayed in the moment, enjoying the simple pleasure an ice cream could provide. He was not a man prone to introspection so this was just another day in his new life - a life with purpose, dedicated to saving one child at a time.

CPSIA information can be obtained
at www.ICGtesting.com
Printed in the USA
BVHW071423250819
556720BV00001B/46/P

9 781644 388693